Corpse of Discovery

A
Portland
Bookmobile
Mystery

B.B. Cantwell

Shilshole Bay Books

Seattle

Portland Bookmobile Mysteries

Murdermobile

Corpse of Discovery

Cover illustration by Stevie Lennartson

Learn more about Portland Bookmobile Mysteries at

murdermobile.weebly.com

For Lillian Freelove

We hope you'll forgive us someday
(we could have gone with Princetta)

Preface

If you lived in Portland, Oregon – or many other parts of the United States – in the late 20th century, you'd likely remember bookmobiles.

These big buses brought entertainment to our doorsteps – or darn close. Every Saturday or so, the bookmobile would lumber up to a nearby park or playground and open its doors to anyone with a library card, whether we were 8 or 80.

It brought tales of faraway lands, ghoulish monsters, fantastic sword fights. It brought romance, history and adventure – before video was something that streamed, before "texting" meant anything more than sitting down with a pen and writing a story.

If you went to grade school in Portland you'd also know the exciting history of Lewis and Clark's Corps of Discovery.

This story weaves all that together – along with quirky tales of the mystical Rajneeshees (who really *did* poison salad bars), miniature horses (which really *are* used as service animals), and wooden shoes (which probably *would* give you blisters if you wore them in a parade). This is, indeed, a work of fiction, but much of it is true.

Oh, there's also a murder. I served on Portland's bookmobile, and I can tell you all about it.

– B.B. Cantwell

Chapter One

Saturday, June 8, 1996
Portland, Oregon

The bookmobile was starting to steam.

"Dagnabit, this is what they get for going cheap and buying this 'reconditioned' thing instead of the new vehicle we were promised," fumed Ethel Pimala, perched behind the wheel of the Miss Sara Duffy Memorial Bookmobile as it crept along Broadway in downtown Portland. The bookmobile driver's years of working with children always showed in her tame cursing.

Just ahead, Corvallis High School's Spartan marching band, in elaborate chrome helmets, tootled away at the "Washington Post March." At least their togas look well-ventilated, thought Hester Freelove McGarrigle, the bookmobile's librarian, wiping a limp wisp of auburn hair from her perspiring brow.

It was an unseasonable scorcher of a June day for the Grand Floral Parade, a highlight of the annual Rose Festival in a town known as Oregon's Rose City. Putting the "new" Portland City Library bookmobile in the parade was the scheme of the publicity-conscious president of the Portland Pioneer Literary Society, the private organization – "our little aristocracy," Hester called it – that contracted with the city to provide library services. The president had crowed to his board that the shiny magenta bus with its supergraphics of the late head librarian, Sara Duffy, reading to a circle of adoring children would be "boffo" exposure for the library.

"Just how well it will play when the bookmobile blows a gasket and they have to send paramedics to rescue us from heat stroke is another question," muttered Hester.

The willowy, blue-eyed "Miss Marple librarian," as the local TV stations had annoyingly dubbed her after her involvement in a local murder investigation, scurried to the rear of the bus a third time to see if she could get the jammed back window to open.

Once more, the library board had buckled to cost constraints and gone with a bookmobile with no air conditioning. Who knew it would be 92 degrees for the Rose Parade? When Hester had agreed to dress up as pioneer Narcissa Whitman in an 1850s-era dress, complete with whalebone corset, she had assumed it would be a typical cool and showery early-June day.

The costume was in keeping with the Rose Festival's theme for this year: "Voyages of Discovery." Keyed to Lewis and Clark's Corps of Discovery and the subsequent history of 19th-century pioneers in what was then called "Oregon Country," the festival encouraged all Portlanders to celebrate their heritage.

"Oh, Pim," Hester called despairingly to her diminutive, somewhat-pineapple-shaped driver whose Filipino-Hawaiian surname, Pimala, was often shortened by friends. "My father, the band teacher, would love this, but if I have to listen to one more John Philip Sousa march, I'm going to tear off this corset and run screaming and naked into Nordstrom's to find some classical piano – and air conditioning!"

Pim, who had come from Hilo decades earlier to study at Portland State University before her scholarship had dried up, waggled the fronds of her woven pandanus-leaf hat, a tribute to the "Kanaka" workers from Hawaii who helped build and run nearby Fort Vancouver, the historic site where Pim volunteered for re-enactments.

"Well, if we can't keep this old bus moving so the fan belt runs faster, you're not the only one who's going to have a breakdown," she warned.

It didn't help that the Literary Society's leader had arranged to have two giant dugout canoes – "just like the ones Lewis and Clark paddled" – strapped atop the bookmobile to add "historic flavor."

"And about 500 more pounds to haul up Broadway," Pim had been grumbling all morning.

Hester remembered with alarm her first car – a stubby little blue Toyota from the 1960s with a high ceiling and truck-sized steering wheel that she had fondly called her "Mr. Magoo car." It had been a good little car except for its penchant for overheating at stoplights on warm days. Just out of library school, she'd spent a year as an elementary-school librarian in the sun-baked Yakima Valley of Washington, where she'd carefully plotted routes to work that allowed her to turn right and circle around a block until a light changed in order to keep air flowing through the radiator.

"Oh, dear. Pim, would it help if we turned on the heater? That's supposed to help drain heat from the engine, isn't it?"

"I've already got it going full blast, and since the only cooling we're getting is from these window-defroster fans, it's getting to be a question of whether this bus melts down first or we do!" Pim replied, reaching down to unbutton the top of her Aloha shirt, part of a collection well-known among her colleagues. Today's was hot pink with hula-dancing tropical fish and scenes of Diamond Head.

Scanning the gauges on the "new" bus – recently retired from Ketchikan, Alaska, one of the few places in the United States where A.C. wouldn't be considered necessary – Pim gave a low whistle.

"We're just edging into the red on the temp gauge. Hester, if this parade doesn't get moving, I'm going to have to take desperate measures."

❖

Leading the parade marched the man responsible for Pim's worries.

Pieter van Dyke, president of the Portland Pioneer Literary Society, was also chairman of the Rose Festival. And chairman of the Oregon Zoo. And vice chairman of the Portland Art Museum. And a socially-climbing member of boards of half a dozen other influential Portland-area community groups, colleges and nonprofits.

In his late 50s, thick-bodied with pouchy eyes and thinning flaxen hair on a head shaped a bit like a tulip bulb, van Dyke today was celebrating his Dutch heritage – and his position as self-appointed grand marshal of the Grand Floral Parade – by marching at its head in wooden shoes.

The impractical footwear was shared by van Dyke's taller, grayer, pinch-faced law partner and fellow Dutchman, DeWitt Vanderpol, limping at his side. Trailing just behind, their baldheaded, bespectacled and plumply unfit junior partner, Gerhard Gerbils, sported lederhosen to reflect his German ancestry. This particular garment fit better in the lawyer's younger days, a few thousand sausages ago. His partners joked that Gerbils' dimpled thighs looked "the wurst for wear."

Gerbils' father had changed the spelling of the family name from "Goebbels" – yes, they *were* related to the infamous Nazi propaganda wizard – when fleeing Germany just before Hitler invaded Poland. Much to his descendants' consternation, old Goebbels simply Anglicized the spelling but kept the pronunciation, with the hard "G," though the new spelling meant his descendants were often mocked as school boys for having the same name as a pet rodent.

Van Dyke and Vanderpol didn't often let their partner forget his distant Nazi relative, smirking together over their private joke the day they appointed Gerbils to handle the firm's public relations.

Gerbils thought their sense of humor mean-spirited.

Today, van Dyke was in his element, waving happily at the crowd lining the curb and beaming with a smile that spoke of dental-chair whitening treatments.

The parade was rounding the block to Fifth Avenue to pass in the shadow of "Portlandia," the 34-foot Statue-of-Liberty-like copper sculpture kneeling over the entry to the neo-art-deco Portland Building. Van Dyke, always hamming it up in public, a habit dating to a high-school role in "Guys and Dolls," threw his hand to his chest and mimicked getting skewered by the giant trident the statue brandished. Onlookers guffawed.

"Wait till they see the bookmobile," he shouted into Vanderpol's ear so as to be heard over the sound of the marching bands. "Getting that reconditioned model left us enough money to hire the airbrush muralist out of Atlanta who does all the fancy graphics on the trucks that carry NASCAR teams. Old Sara Duffy never looked so good!" he said of the elderly librarian, the victim in the murder case Hester had helped solve. "That little glint in her eye? The guy actually uses diamond dust to get that effect!"

The grandson of Vincent van Dyke, a former governor and subsequent Oregon Supreme Court justice, Pieter van Dyke had grown up watching his father, Vincent Jr. – also a lawyer – unsuccessfully run for one public office after another. Pieter's basic life strategy was to glad-hand his way into the public's heart. He had a reputation for throwing Portland's most lavish high-society parties, including hosting the annual Friends of the Library New Year's Costume Ball, the group's premier fundraiser. Pieter always dressed as Pierrot.

"Speaking of the good old book bus, I wonder where it ended up in the parade? I told them to put it near the front," van Dyke told Vanderpol, as both peered over their shoulders.

❖

Watching the bookmobile's temperature needle climb every time the hot engine idled, Pim was sweating from nerves as much as from the heat.

"I've got to keep this thing moving and keep that fan spinning or she's going to boil over for sure!" she told Hester. "Hold on, I'm going through the marching band!"

"Pim, be careful!" Hester grimaced, covering her eyes with both hands.

Pim, who had been driving for the library for 40 years, gently goosed the accelerator and the bookmobile edged toward the waddling derrières of the Spartan band's tuba section. Then fate took a hand. It was time for the band's special drill, and as the drum major's whistle shrieked, the band members pivoted to march backward, aiming straight for the oncoming 12-ton bus, whose magenta hue – the favorite color of Portland's first head librarian – made it hard to miss.

Pim flashed the high beams through a cloud of steam and Hester waved her long arms like a Navy signal officer working the semaphore.

The drum major – a quick-thinking member of the Math Club – nodded his high, plumed hat, shrilled his whistle three times and waggled arms in his own special code as the band magically parted on each side of the big bus. Pistoning trombone slides narrowly missed the rearview mirrors. Pim hit the air horn in rhythm to the band's march – Hester recognized "Stars and Stripes Forever" – and the crowd cheered at what looked like a planned bit of choreography.

But disaster loomed.

"Pim, look out, the sheriff's horse patrol is stopped in front of us!" Hester warned.

"I will not be a horse murderer!" Pim said grimly. Her love of animals started at home with her ancient cockapoo, Queen Liliuokalani.

"Quick, take this right turn and maybe we can circle around the block and rejoin the parade after this thing has cooled off a bit!" Hester coached.

"Just like in your old Magoo car!" Pim grinned, gunning the engine. Giving it all the leverage her 4-foot-10 physique could muster, she cranked the wheel to swing the lumbering vehicle onto Yamhill Street.

City father Simon Benson wanted Portland to be walkable, so downtown blocks were platted half the size of city blocks in New York.

"Pim, we're going to need to go several streets over if you really want to give the fan time to cool down this beast," opined Hester, leaning out the open passenger window in an effort to get some fresh air. She reached up and yanked out a pearl-handled hair pin so her coppery tresses fell out of the pioneer bun and caught the breeze.

Glancing in the bus's side mirror and catching a reflection of her own slim face with strong cheekbones straining for the air currents, she suddenly felt like one of those floppy-eared dogs who just love to go for rides.

"And I don't give a hoot!" she thought, relishing the few cooling freshets.

Pim leaned on the horn, ran yellow lights and sent more than one baby-jogger-pushing mother scurrying for the curb. Hester, peering down side streets, finally glimpsed the parade where it had turned a corner and headed back on a parallel course.

"Pim, hang a left, I think there's an opening for us!"

The big bus bobbed and swayed, and as it leaned around the corner a few unsecured books flew from the mystery shelves.

"OK, the needle's dropped, thank you Goddess Pele!" said Pim, addressing the sky. "And look ahead up there at the parade, Hester, that looks like the Allee-ANCE Fran-SAY fur trappers from over at the fort," she added, tackling the re-enactment group's name with her usual exaggerated diction reserved for tweaking what she called "them highfalutin' languages."

"Oh, are those the fellows you know from the historical park? Do you think they'll let us barge in?"

"Sure, that's my buddy Pomp Charbonneau leading them! He's a direct descendant of one of the Lewis and Clark gang. He was the guy who helped me print up those fliers for the Kanaka Village fundraising picnic. Remember, you met him that once."

Leading two columns of unshaven men in buckskin breeches was a wiry, raven-bearded Gaul in an eye-catching raccoon hat. And this wasn't just the raccoon's *tail* – it was a whole taxidermied raccoon, wrapped around his head. As he waved the tricolor flag of Napoleon, Pomp Charbonneau's green eyes danced and the raccoon's shiny marble eyes bobbed above. Its little paws waved as if in a plea for help.

"My God!" Hester recoiled.

❖

Oh, boy, is the captain going to owe me for this, Nate Darrow kept telling himself as sweat stains spread up the side of his T-shirt under the blazing sun. Across the back was the slogan "Hopped Up on Full Sail IPA," an homage to his favorite Columbia Gorge craft brewer.

Portland might get rain and ice in the winter, but it could also get beastly hot in the summer, Darrow had been warned as he headed into his first June in the city, after moving north from the university town of Eugene. Rivers bring some breezes, but Portland is 100 miles up the Columbia River from the cooling ocean air.

But this was too early for this kind of heat, everyone agreed.

As the new guy in the Portland Police Bureau detective squad – and one of few who'd come up through the ranks and had memories of "those good ol' days of traffic duty," he'd been reminded – Darrow had been "volunteered" to help supervise in staging the parade, one of his captain's favorite public-service projects.

Darrow expected it also had something to do with his "rising star" having risen too fast in his first months, when the press overplayed his part in "single-handedly" reviving the bookmobile librarian after she'd fainted at finding a body in her bookmobile.

For this one day, it meant he was organizing 15 traffic cops, a half dozen bike patrolmen, eight meter maids, and even the horse patrol.

Finally the first part of the parade had reached the end point, where Taylor Street crossed over the Stadium Freeway. The tall detective, with a runner's build and a prematurely graying thatch of hair over luxuriant chestnut eyebrows and a strong aquiline nose, watched with satisfaction as a stocky, baldheaded uniformed cop in aviator sunglasses furiously waved the Rose Queen float into a church parking lot.

In the First Aid tent at the lot's edge, two red-faced and grimacing men in their 50s were prying off wooden shoes as they showed a nurse their blisters.

The brassy notes of a Sousa march wafted up the block. But another sound clashed in Darrow's ear, causing him to turn and look back down Taylor. There in the middle of the parade, a buckskin-clad man with a wild animal on his head waved his arms like a band conductor and split the ranks of mountain men marching behind him.

And through the middle came the new Sara Duffy Memorial Bookmobile, its air horn blaring as if it were a fogbound freighter crossing the Columbia River bar.

As Darrow stared with dropped jaw the big bus ground to a halt 10 feet away. Clouds of steam fogged its windows.

The front door popped open and Hester McGarrigle, her face red as a beet, stumbled to the pavement.

Seeing Darrow, she started to speak, but all that came out was a squeak. Her eyes rolled back in her head and she slumped in a faint just as Nate Darrow rushed forward to catch her.

"Oh, Ms. McGarrigle, we really need to stop meeting this way," he said under his breath as he carried Hester to the First Aid tent.

Chapter Two

S unday and Monday were the bookmobile crew's customary days off, so there was plenty of time to recover from the heat. This morning, Pim was hot under the collar for a different reason.

"Why do they have to change our route? It was perfectly fine just as it was, and anytime they change it to make things more 'efficient' " – she curled her stubby fingers in air quotes – "it just confuses the patrons and we show up at stops with nobody there!"

"And it complicates my job because I don't know who's going to show up at a new stop and what they might like to read," Hester added. Unlike a regular library, the bookmobile catered to specific patrons on its different runs. Sometimes that meant stocking up on romances and westerns, or filling the shelves with movie-star biographies. Today Hester had tried to shelve a broader selection, including some young-adult novels in hopes of snagging a teen reader or two. "I can always dream!" she told Pim.

The librarian suspected her driver's ire had to do with more than just the reading public, however. The change of stops also meant Madame Pim wouldn't get to have lunch at the Onion-Aire burger stand by the Skyline bookmobile stop every Tuesday, Hester mused, suppressing a smile.

The Onion-Aire's regular burgers came with two hefty beef patties, and Pim's normal order was for an extra patty on top of that. The café had a standing challenge that if you ordered a burger with four patties – a Walla Walla Whomper – and finished it in one sitting, they'd give you another free. It was one of Pim's long-standing ambitions.

"But then she'd explode," Hester said to herself.

"What's that you say?" Pim asked.

"Oh!" Hester looked up as Pim parked at the Skyline stop at 9 a.m., the new scheduled time for the hilltop lookout, which today was wrapped in thick fog. "Uh, I was just thanking our lucky stars this old bus didn't explode coming up the hill. After it got so overheated in the parade."

"Yeah, well, Bob Newall said he spent all day yesterday flushing out the radiator; he practically flooded the bookmobile barn," Pim said, referring to the long-suffering mechanic who kept Portland's Mobile Library Unit chugging along. "And I didn't waste my days off. It gave me time to catch up on the Rose Medallion clues. Me and Millie Eubanks from the motor pool – you know that gal who almost got on 'Jeopardy'? – we're putting our heads together and I think we have a chance at it. And it comes with big bucks this time, did you hear?"

The Rose Medallion search was a longstanding, highly popular part of Rose Festival. Every June, a small bronze medallion about the size of an Olympic medal and engraved with a rosebud was hidden "in plain sight," as contest organizers put it, somewhere around Portland. Clues to its whereabouts were published each morning in *The Oregonian* newspaper, starting out very vaguely and getting more obvious as the week wore on. Whoever was first to find the medallion won all sorts of donated prizes.

This year, in celebration of its 50th year in business, a local manufacturer of sport runners, Zeus Shoes, had put up $50,000 cash, stoking interest to a fevered pitch.

"That would sure put a nice bump in the double-wide fund," Pim said with a wink over the top of her cateye glasses. Pim lived along the pretty Sandy River in an aging, mossy single-wide trailer house on 10 acres, part of a long-ago divorce settlement. She often complained of being "land rich."

As Pim finished setting up the Instie-Circ, the portable circulation computer, Hester put out the step by the bookmobile's rear door and waved through the murky mist to the day's first patron, Mrs. Loman, who was just coming into focus down the walk with her customary two shopping bags of library books, one in each arm. Hester liked to think the bags acted as ballast to keep the wispy octogenarian from blowing away on the hilltop's gusty winds.

Mrs. Loman's sweet nature belied an insatiable appetite for murder mysteries. Hester reached into a cupboard for the new J.A. Jance she had saved for her favorite patron, who rewarded Hester with a smile made even wider by a pair of ill-fitting dentures.

"Did you see us in the parade, Mrs. L?" Pim asked, almost shouting to compensate for Mrs. Loman's hearing loss.

"What's that? I'm fine if you don't mumble, dear," she warbled.

"Parade! Parade!" Pim bellowed.

"Oh, I love charades!" she said, looking slightly befuddled. "Is the library having another Seniors Parlor Game Night?"

Hester smiled, nodded and handed Mrs. Loman a library events calendar.

Next to climb aboard were the Donaldson sisters, identical twins, both widowed in their late 60s, who dressed alike and lately had taken to checking out books with one another's library cards in a giggly effort to trick Hester.

Behind them, a recent new patron at this stop was Mr. O'Leary, a recently retired accountant and self-proclaimed "available specimen" with too much time on his hands who was making a study of mathematician biographies.

"Hullo, Hester," he said through his walrus mustache, its tips waxed to a point. "I saw the trouble you had in the parade. The TV said the bookmobile almost took out an entire high-school class!"

"Well, it really wasn't like that, you know how they exaggerate," she said, giving him her "Hester Sunshine" voice.

"And they're saying now that it has to do with that van Dyke, that there's some sort of investigation of how he's mishandled library funds. I guess he was supposed to use a bunch of donated money to buy you gals a brand-spanking new bus, not this tarted up old thing, eh?"

"Oh, I wouldn't know about that," Hester said, handing him a biography of Alexandre Grothendieck, father of the Theory of Schemes, which Mr. O'Leary had ordered on interlibrary loan from Boston Public Library. It was the only known copy in North America.

Hester had been doing her best in recent weeks to divert this overly attentive patron's attentions to the Donaldson sisters, who were known, as Pim put it, "to take a shine to anything in long trousers." But every time Hester delivered a special book he ordered, O'Leary acted as if she had done him a personal favor. The red-faced little man ordered special books all the time.

"Oh, my favorite librarian in the world has another prize for me!" O'Leary brayed, with both chins wagging. "Thank you, Saint Hester!"

Hester sighed deeply, readjusted the nametag pinned to her sweater and suddenly busied herself helping a young mother with a 2-year-old in a tie-dyed onesie over by the children's shelves.

"Let's get moving, Pim, before Mr. Mustachio comes back," Hester hissed a half-hour later as she pulled in the step. "I swear, I'm going to have to ask Bob to fumigate this thing with Pine-Sol to get rid of the curse of Aramis. He must bathe in the stuff."

The fog that wrapped the city was a welcome cooling agent after the weekend's heat. And it was persistent. Pim leaned over the big steering wheel to peer through the windshield. She flicked the wipers to squeal across the moist glass a few times as they made their way slowly downhill to a new stop edging Forest Park in Northwest Portland.

"I'm glad I studied my Thomas Guide to get us to this new spot, 'cuz this pea soup sure as heck-fire isn't helping," said Pim, never losing a chance to sing the praises of the map book that she called her Bookmobile Bible. "But I sure wish the siting committee would drive out to these spots before sending us to the back of beyond. Look at this!"

Pim was carefully threading the big bus down a narrow street with just enough room between solid rows of parked cars to squeak through if ...

"Nope, can't do it, hang on a second!" Pim clucked as she yanked on the parking brake, leapt from her seat, barreled out the rear door, ran to the front and folded in both side mirrors, then scuffled back to her driver's seat.

"OK, now I think we can make it, but where we're going to park down here, Jumping Jehosephat knows!"

Hester studied the "Location Information Missive" that had been sent along by Dora, the library's bookkeeper and "Head Bossy Boots," as Pim called her. Dora's "missives" were supposed to tell where it was OK for the bookmobile to park and turn around at each designated stop.

"It says something in hieroglyphics here about 'Horseshoe pt. OK 4 pkg. Posts hv. bn. remved.' But I haven't a clue what that means," Hester groaned as Pim came to the road's end. "Why does she have to write these instructions like she's a code specialist moving a MASH unit into enemy territory?"

Above them, a high, arching bridge soared above the park entrance and carried Thurman Street to the upper west side of town. A walkway from the road's end threaded beneath the bridge and followed a stream reputed for its resident trout population. On weekend mornings, the path transported legions of joggers and dog-walkers into the huge wooded preserve, known as the nation's largest park inside city boundaries.

Just ahead of the bookmobile a narrow driveway led to a building with restrooms.

"Well, this is just dandy, folks, how am I supposed to turn this thing around?" Pim blustered as the big bus ground to a halt. But not one to be daunted by any challenge, she immediately ground the gears, inched forward and started maneuvering up and back in what turned into a 16-point turn to get the bookmobile facing the other direction.

Only once did Hester wince when a corner of the front bumper pulled a branch off a little ginkgo tree "planted by Mrs. Rasmussen's Third Grade Class in honor of the Challenger astronauts," according to a plaque.

"OK, now where do we park so we're not in the way? I can't really see a dang thing in this fog, but it looks like there's a sandy area there next to the restrooms that could take us. I'm backing in!" Pim declared, jumping out of her seat to unfold the mirrors again.

"Aha, Pim – sandy area? Could it be a horseshoe pit? I think I just made sense of Dora's gibberish!" Hester laughed when her driver climbed back in her seat. "And it says the iron posts have been removed so we're good to go!"

As she steered by the mirrors, there was a moment when the big bus seemed to stall, but Pim "just gunned it," as she liked to say, and the bookmobile bumped and swayed to a resting point.

Only a few patrons found them this first day in the new stop, but Hester was happy to check out a copy of "Treasure Island" to a shy 10-year-old boy and the latest Thomas Jefferson biography to his father.

Like a theater curtain rising, the fog finally lifted. A cloud of blue smoke took its place as Pim revved the diesel and readied for departure. Just as Hester opened the rear door to pull up the portable step, she looked up into the smiling face of a runner in an Oregon Ducks sweatshirt, his thighs sheathed in tight green nylon running shorts.

"Hester, what the heck are you doing here?" asked a panting and sweaty Nate Darrow, the police detective who lived upstairs from her in an apartment building less than a mile away.

"Oh, Nate! This is where you go trail-running! Of course!"

As was often the case when she unexpectedly ran into her neighbor, she found herself blushing, which she never could quite explain. Frankly, it was getting a little irritating.

"It's a new bookmobile stop, our first day here," she finally blurted in answer to his question, forcing her eyes away from the tan, muscled calves that Darrow was now leaning over to massage.

Too late. His eye caught hers.

"Sorry, I've been cramping up for no good reason, for the last three miles," he said through gritted teeth.

"What, you've been running half-naked in a cold and penetrating fog of which Dickens would be proud and you can't figure out why your muscles are knotting up?" Hester asked.

Darrow shot her a look.

"Anyway, you're just in time to help guide us out of here, if you'd be so kind," Hester chirped, happy to regain her equilibrium. "Pim is a little worried about getting stuck in this darn sand."

Darrow waved them ahead as Pim slowly eased the bus forward, but again it hung up halfway along and the engine stalled. Pim cranked it back to life, then gradually eased out the clutch. With another bounce and jounce, they cleared the sand.

Hester stuck her head out the side window to thank Darrow, but suddenly she couldn't see him. "Where the heck did he go, Pim?"

She got up and trotted to the rear door, swung it open and hopped out to see Darrow staring at the sand pit behind the bookmobile.

He looked up at her as if he'd seen a ghost.

"Oh my God, not again, Hester," he croaked.

He stepped forward to stop her, but she turned and got a quick glimpse of Pieter van Dyke, nude except for his tidy-whitie Fruit of the Looms, spread-eagled in the sand. His hands and feet were duct-taped to horseshoe posts pounded deep into the ground.

Tire tracks edged one side of his tubby torso, and his eyes stared sightlessly into the now-blue June sky.

Chapter Three

For the second time in four months, yellow police-line tape surrounded Portland's magenta bookmobile. But to Hester McGarrigle's eye, there was nothing cheery about the complementary colors.

Sitting in the passenger seat of a parked police cruiser, she now noticed an old wooden sign next to the horseshoe pit proclaiming it one of the practice sites for the venerable Rose City Horseshoe Club ("Est. 1922"). In the sign's center, an elaborate logo featured a horseshoe intertwined with a vine of red roses. The police car's endlessly strobing red and blue lights reflected off the sign and, next to it, the bookmobile's bright finish.

"Nobody better be epileptic or they'll have a fit for sure," she complained through a grating to Pim, who occupied the cruiser's back seat. "It's worse than a disco ball in the Jelly Belly factory. I wonder if I could turn them off?" she pondered, lightly fingering a panel of switches beneath the car's dashboard.

"Hester, don't go punching any buttons and getting us in worse trouble than we already are!" Pim whispered in agitation. "Unless you see one marked 'ejector seat.' These back seats aren't exactly made for full-figured gals."

Hester chuckled nervously, then took a deep breath and blew it out with a "whoosh."

"Oh, God, Pim, how could this have happened – again?" she asked, bunching a fist to her mouth.

The previous February, Hester had been the first to discover the body of the retired head librarian, Sara Duffy, in the bookmobile's back cupboard. After finally confessing, the murderer drove the old bus off a cliff. The replacement bus was named in Duffy's honor.

Hester shuddered at the memories. Squeezing her eyes shut, she tried to process this morning's events. When she looked up again, Detective Darrow was just opening the car door to slip into the driver's seat. He had found some rain pants in the cruiser's trunk and borrowed a nylon jacket, navy blue with large yellow letters on the back spelling P-O-L-I-C-E.

"So, you two," he said, pursing his lips and staring through the windshield at the densely wooded ridge rising abruptly above the industry-lined Willamette River. Along the ridgeline the top branches of myriad fir trees formed an inky, dark filigree pattern against blue sky. Darrow drummed his fingers on the dashboard.

Hester looked at him with searching eyes. "Nate, uh, did the bookmobile actually… "

Darrow spoke quickly and matter-of-factly.

"There's clear evidence that one set of rear dual tires ran over the victim. It's by no means clear whether that caused his death. There's a lot of blood in the sand and a lot of sand caked on the body. The medical examiner is doing a preliminary look now."

Hester's breath whistled between her teeth. In the rear of the car, Pim was moaning softly and holding her head in her hands.

"Pim, there was no way you could have seen him, it was way too murky out there," Hester comforted.

Darrow hung his head for a moment and then looked up at Hester.

"Look, I'm sorry you both have to go through all this again, but I think it would be best if you went into the office and gave your statements there," he said, watching in a mirror as a KSNZ News van pulled onto the grass next to the trail and a crew quickly raised a satellite dish atop the roof. Darrow recognized reporter Misty Day as she peered at her reflection in the van's passenger window and applied fresh coral-colored lipstick.

Darrow also noted with some concern that quite a crowd had gathered at the outer perimeter of the police tape. He momentarily noticed that their expressions went beyond the usual morbid curiosity common to a murder scene, instead bordering on ... indignation?

Several waved folded newspapers. What was up with that?

In answer, there came a sudden tapping on the car window. Darrow lowered the window to his plainclothes colleague, Harry Harrington, a slightly built man of conservative dress whose demeanor tended to alternate between inexplicable optimist and hopeless worry wart. A wave of coffee breath filled the car as Harrington leaned in a little too far and hissed some news that Hester couldn't help overhearing.

"Nate, we got trouble! I know this sounds crazy, but there's a whole passel of maniacs out there who insist that the Rose Medallion is hidden in that damn horseshoe pit! They say there's hardly any doubt from the clue in this morning's paper. Look at this!"

Darrow took the newspaper Harrington thrust at him and peered at some circled text:

Gallop north by Nor'west to a park called For-est.
Beneath Thurman Bridge find a pit, not a ridge.
Don't get sand in your eyes when you pick up the prize.

Pim, her interest in the world around her suddenly revived, spoke up from the back seat.

"Is that today's *Oregonian*? Can I have a look? I couldn't find a copy for love nor money this morning!"

"Nobody could – not until about an hour ago. They had some sort of press breakdown. But now we're getting mobbed by frustrated medallion hunters!" Harrington moaned. "What are we supposed to do? These people are fanatics!"

Darrow shook his head.

"That could mean any number of things, for God's sake. Harry, just be sure we have enough uniforms to keep the turkeys out of our crime scene. Call for more backup, why don't you?"

Chapter Four

Misty Day had never had to change her name from Gladys Frump or Mabel Crumb; the precious name her parents had given her was perfect for TV. She grew up as a cheerleader, a natural blond and a Beaverton High School valedictorian. She'd kept her figure thanks to Thighmaster, Lean Cuisine and ordering salad dressing "on the side" ever since Jimmy Carter was president. As for her still-yellow tresses? Only her hairdresser knew for sure.

She had known her days were numbered as co-anchor at Portland's No. 2-rated network affiliate when they hired a news director half her age – "younger than sperm," she called the young buck fresh out of USC.

And sure enough, not a week after her 50th birthday, he'd taken her out for lunch for the "it's time to put you back on the beat" talk.

Between the Chilean sea bass and the tiramisu, he'd shoveled flattery about how her "seasoned eye" and keen sense of "the pulse of Portland" made her the right person to do a series of people profiles they would call Misty's Mavens.

But the other shoe dropped when she learned who was taking her place at the anchor desk: an oh-so-perky 29-year-old former weather girl in a push-up bra whose "hard news" claim to fame was an exposé on pet psychics.

So Day was hungry for a story that would help restore gravitas to her curriculum vitae.

"And being first on air with another high-profile homicide on the Murdermobile sounds like just the thing," she said out loud, giving each word a snap like a staple-gun as she trotted toward Detective Darrow at the edge of Forest Park. He had just waved off a squad car that was threading its way along the narrow street back toward downtown.

She didn't wait for any preliminaries but signaled her cameraman to roll video as she thrust her microphone in Darrow's face.

"Detective, is it true that the 'Murdermobile' is back, and this time its victim is the head of the Portland Pioneer Literary Society?"

Darrow, caught off-guard, turned toward the camera with a look as if he'd just stepped in something he didn't like the smell of. But Day didn't wait for him to respond.

"And is it true that Pieter van Dyke was not only run over by the bookmobile but was stripped naked and tortured in some sort of satanic cult ritual?"

"WHAT?" Darrow spluttered. He hated being on TV. He always ended up looking like Eddie Haskell from "Leave it to Beaver" – if you added a 5 o'clock shadow – and sounding like Barney Fife. It just wasn't his medium.

"And that librarian just taken away in the patrol car – Heather Freelove Something, wasn't it? Is she part of the 'free love' cult out on Sauvie Island?" Day added.

Darrow managed to snap his jaw shut rather than let it hang in response to the preposterous questions.

"NO, we have no – " he stopped to draw a breath " – no positive ID of the victim. And no comment in this early stage of the investigation," he said, biting off the urge to bite the reporter's head off. It would only fuel her fire.

But that didn't stop Misty Day, who just gave him a smirking, "Thanks, Nick."

Licking her lips and dropping the microphone to her side, she looked him up and down. "Hey, haven't we passed each other on morning runs up here? I seem to remember some tight green shorts."

Darrow just stared back at her under eyebrows like gathering storm clouds until she waved her cameraman over to the horseshoe pit and quickly positioned herself for a stand-up. A pair of white-shirted EMTs with a gurney was preparing to load a body bag into the medical examiner's windowless white van. After catching that wide shot, the cameraman zoomed in on four horseshoe posts, sunk deeply in the sand

and still bearing hanks of duct tape, and a large dark stain marking where the body had lain between them. Next he zoomed out to focus on the reporter as she launched into her commentary.

"So, this is Misty Day, asking questions with no answers – *just yet*. But I knew Pieter van Dyke personally. I lunched with him just last week – paella in the Pearl District. You all saw him lead the Rose Parade days ago in his charming wooden shoes. Somehow this minion of Portland society has apparently met an ignoble death here, in some sort of bizarre ritual. For months, our chief of police has been harping about the petty crime wave in this corner of Portland, with several arrests of residents of Downward Dog Farm, the Rajneeshee spinoff commune on nearby Sauvie Island. Now, has this cult's disrespect for the rule of law turned deadly, targeting one of our most prominent civic leaders? I, for one, won't rest until questions are answered. I'm Misty Day, for KSNZ News You Can Use."

Darrow had learned the hard way that trying to correct the wild ideas that some TV reporters tended to sling about like gravy on Thanksgiving was about as easy as, well, getting a gravy stain off a silk tie. He turned to face a problem he could do something about: the crowd of onlookers who were starting to hop the police tape. He grabbed a bullhorn from the trunk of Harry Harrington's unmarked blue Caprice.

"Hey, hey, folks, let us do our job here, this is a crime scene and we will be here all day, so please just go home," Darrow beseeched, his amplified words echoing with a tinny vibrato through the little canyon beneath the bridge.

"But I was here first and if I could just look for the Rose Medallion for two minutes I promise I won't touch anything," pleaded a young mother in Coke-bottle eyeglasses and chestnut braids with a crying baby in a knitted bag strapped to her chest.

"NO, I'M SORRY – " Darrow stopped and lowered the bullhorn as the baby's cries turned to shrieks. "I'm sorry," he said in a muted voice. "We have what looks to be a homicide here. It has to take priority, I'm sure you understand. Please just go home."

Darrow hadn't had any coffee before setting out for his morning run, so now his head was pounding from caffeine withdrawal. Added to the charley-horse in his right calf, he was gimping about like Long John Silver after a hard night of pillaging. He staggered over to his fellow detective.

"Harry, it looks like the crime-scene folks and the extra uniforms can handle this now. How about giving me a lift back downtown?" he asked. "I need to interview a librarian I know."

❖

DeWitt Vanderpol had just turned off the television and was on the phone to his law partner, Gerhard Gerbils.

"Why do *I* have to be the one to make a statement about his death?" Gerbils asked, not trying to conceal a prickly tone.

"Because you're the firm's spokesman, remember?" said Vanderpol, who did his best to conceal a lifelong fear of public speaking which he had hoped to overcome by becoming a lawyer.

"I just think you knew him better, you worked with him longer, and besides, I'm the junior partner, which means you get 5 percent more of the firm's gross than I do," Gerbils added snarkily. Suddenly, something dawned on him. "So…now that Pieter is gone, shouldn't we just split things 50-50?"

"It's way too early to be thinking of anything like that!" Vanderpol snapped. "But we just lost our biggest link to the community. There may not be anything left to split unless we're way out in front on this – 'what a tragedy it is, but we'll continue serving our loyal clients, it's what he'd want,' all that kind of stuff. I called the police chief and he expects to have a press briefing tomorrow. I told him we'd be there."

❖

Pomp Charbonneau plopped down in the dinette of his travel trailer, the cushions draped with a French tricolor afghan knitted by Wife No. 2, and munched on a snack of brie and Triscuits as he paused to admire the new antelope head mounted above his portable television. He saw no need to tell anyone it was road kill from an unfortunate accident he'd had driving across Malheur National Wildlife Refuge on a recent trip to southeastern Oregon.

He flipped on KSNZ news in the hope of catching that foxy new anchor girl. So much better than the old bag she replaced. And he always had an eye out for the "next former Mrs. Charbonneau," as he liked to call his romantic conquests.

There she was!

"Oh, my heart goes pitty pat, mon cheri!" he cooed, holding up his wineglass in salute and waggling the other hand over his chest. She was introducing a news story.

"And now we have a live report from veteran reporter Misty Day at the scene of the apparent murder of Portland civic leader Pieter van Dyke, on the edge of Forest Park. Misty?"

Charbonneau's head jerked as if he'd been slapped the way Wife No. 3 used to do. His wineglass dropped and shattered, soaking a rug with several ounces of a very nice Sancerre.

On rural Sauvie Island, 10 miles northwest of downtown, the Portland area's most famous nude beach was sprinkled with its usual cross-section of patchouli-scented hippie women, aging gay men and grizzled old bikers with more faded tattoos than anyone ever wanted to see. As usual, binocular-toting crews on heavily laden container ships plodding up the Columbia River crowded the starboard railing to get a look at their next port of call – and anything else they could see.

Mostly farmland and wildlife refuge, the island was where Hester's parents had taken her as a child to pick pumpkins at Halloween. Her mother had delighted in spying for migrating buffleheads and mergansers there with her Audubon chapter while her father explored the back roads with his teachers' cycling group.

Down the road from the nude beach, it was another sunny June day at Downward Dog Farm. Ma Anand Martha was out in the farmyard petting the chickens, each of whom had a name and none of whom would ever be slaughtered.

Downward Dog Farm had some of the oldest chickens in Oregon. What it didn't have was a television.

Chapter Five

"**S**o everyone's favorite Channel 3 reporter is convinced you're part of the old Rajneeshee commune because of your middle name," Darrow told Hester two hours later in an interrogation room at Portland Police Bureau headquarters.

"Oh my sainted aunt!" said Hester, slapping her chest with a half-stifled snort. "Well, actually, she *was* my sainted aunt, old Freelove Princetta McGarrigle, of Nova Scotia, from whom my parents got my adorable middle name. As I've told anyone who has ever asked, it's one of the old-fashioned virtue names, like Faith, Hope and Charity."

"Yes, I remember," Darrow said, "and your first name comes from the writings of Nathaniel Hawthorne, for whom I was named." Their eyes locked for a long moment.

"You two gonna sing a duet or something?" Pim asked, looking worriedly back and forth at them.

The moment's spell broken, Darrow handed Hester some coffee in a cracked red mug that he'd brought in from the staff room, and handed a cracked blue mug to Pim, who sat silently glowering at him from the other end of the table. The smell of steaming Maxwell House competed with the room's permanent aroma of old socks. "And forgive me for not correcting Misty Day at the time, but my experience is that you can always tell a TV reporter – "

"But you can't tell them much," Hester finished the old saying for him with a groan and a grin. "My father says that about Scotsmen, which is allowed since he is one."

"Yes, my dad used to say it about Swedes, since we had a few in the family," Darrow said, leaning back in an orange plastic chair that reminded him of his high-school cafeteria, and putting his feet up on the table as he used to do in his high-school cafeteria.

The table was old, wooden and covered with scribbled graffiti. "Jim Bob + Mr. T, 1989," scrawled in black Sharpie, caught Hester's eye.

"So, as enchanting as I find your workplace, Mr. Darrow, how soon can Pim and I be on our way?" she asked.

"Yes, I'd like to know that, too, Inspector, whenever you're done with your screen test for 'Fast Times at Ridgemont High,'" added Pim, reverting to her favorite sarcastic name for the policeman who had helped mistakenly send her to jail a few months earlier as a suspect in Sara Duffy's murder. She had never warmed to him.

Darrow gazed silently at Pim for two beats, then gave her a wink before continuing.

"Well, I'm sorry it took so long, but I just got word from the Medical Examiner confirming what I suspected: that Mr. van Dyke had expired hours before the bookmobile ever arrived this morning."

"Oh, thank goodness," Hester blurted, then stopped. "I mean, that's terrible, what happened – but it means..."

"It means Ethel won't be charged with anything, because there's not a lot of interest at the prosecutor's office in trying someone for manslaughter when the victim was already dead," Darrow finished her thought.

"Well, duh," Pim said. "So can we go now?"

Darrow held her gaze again.

"Just tell me this, both of you. Did you see *anything* unusual when you were backing into that horseshoe pit this morning?"

Pim hung her head as she searched her memory.

"Fact is, it was white-out fog down in that gully, probably as bad as I've ever seen fog anytime, anywhere. So I was real careful and took it dead slow – oh, maybe that's a bad choice of words. But if you go too slowly in that darned bus it tends to die on you – oh, oops again. And that infernal backup beeper was going, so loud as to wake the dead – "

Hester quickly interrupted.

"What Pim is saying is that she took all due diligence to carefully maneuver the bookmobile into the new parking spot to which we'd been assigned, and we saw nothing out of the ordinary considering the extraordinarily difficult conditions."

She stopped, with her chin in the air, before continuing hesitantly.

"So, since it thankfully wasn't the bookmobile, what *was* the cause of death, may I ask?"

Darrow glanced at the two-way mirror on the wall, sipped at his own mug of coffee, and decided he didn't care if his partner – or even his impossible-to-please Capt. Myerson – thought he was telling too much.

"Well, I'd say it was the bullet hole right there," he answered, putting his index finger over his heart. "All the sand tended to obscure it at first."

Hester and Pim both gasped.

"But there's another weird thing about all this – besides the head of the library society being shot and left spread-eagled in his undies in a city park's horseshoe pit. And that's the Rose Medallion."

Pim jumped as if stricken. "Did someone find it?"

"Pim's been hot on the trail all week," Hester confided.

It was Darrow's turn to be surprised.

"Oh, really? Well, as you witnessed, we had a small army of medallion searchers out at the crime scene this morning, and now *The Oregonian* has confirmed it: The Rose Medallion was stuck to the logo on the Horseshoe Club sign."

Pim swooned.

"Oh, no! You mean I could have practically grabbed it from the window of the bookmobile this morning?"

Darrow gave her a deadpan face. He took a sip of coffee and waited two beats before continuing.

"So neither of you saw it?"

Pim raised her eyes to the ceiling and clapped her hands with a loud pop. "Don't you think I'd be over at the Zeus Shoes headquarters claiming the $50,000 right now if I had?"

Darrow curled his lower lip as he rocked the old chair back and forth on two legs, then came back down with a thump as he spoke.

"Well, the interesting thing is, the medallion is gone."

Chapter Six

C hief Charles Morse came to the Portland Police Bureau by way of appointment by Mayor Buzz Brinkley, the so-called "People's Mayor," the handlebar-mustachioed owner of a Hawthorne-district brewpub who rode his old balloon-tire bicycle to City Hall every day.

Morse, a potato-nosed, acne-scarred bureaucratic tyrant whose political bent was more NRA than ACLU, was Mayor Buzz's attempt to succor the law-and-order crowd.

Early Wednesday morning Morse was standing at the mahogany dais in the Police Bureau's auditorium at Second Avenue and Main Street and briefing the press on the investigation of Pieter van Dyke's murder.

A former chief in the Columbia Gorge city of The Dalles, Oregon, Morse had spent much of his career focused on – some said obsessed with – the 1980s takeover of parts of Central Oregon by the followers of the Indian mystic Bhagwan Shree Rajneesh.

Among other misadventures, the Rajneeshees had infamously poisoned more than 700 people in The Dalles by tainting salad bars with salmonella in an effort to reduce voter turnout in a local election in which the cult was trying to pack the county courthouse with its own members. (The scheme also involved spreading pathogens on the handles of courthouse urinals.)

The election ploy flopped. But Charles Morse never again trusted anyone in water-buffalo sandals.

"With this horrendous, ritualistic murder of one of Portland's finest citizens, we will look very closely at cults and anyone who practices strange and godless rituals," Morse said, a droplet of perspiration on his

31

ruddy cheek suggesting that his woolen dress uniform with the stiff shoulder-boards and "scrambled eggs" on its brimmed hat was perhaps not the best choice for a heavyset man in a crowded, poorly ventilated room full of klieg lights.

"Chief, is it not correct that the former Rajneeshees at Downward Dog Farm on Sauvie Island are the focus of your investigation?" asked Misty Day, whose tightly French-knotted hair today seemed to pull the darkly tanned skin on her temples even tauter than her plastic surgeon had intended.

Morse squared his jaw and nodded.

"Any group whose history shows a blatant disregard for the health of the Oregon public will certainly be spotlighted by our intensive investigation, and this particular community has recently been involved in a series of shoplifting incidents in Northwest Portland, along with aggressive panhandling involving threatening use of finger cymbals."

Nate Darrow, leaning against a doorjamb at the back of the room, ground his teeth over the chief's blind-spot on anything remotely related to the Rajneeshees. And this blond bimbo from Channel 3 was just making things worse.

Morse, after pausing to take a long gulp from a glass of ice water, continued.

"Now I'd like to allow a representative from the victim's law firm to say a word."

Today, Gerhard Gerbils' gray pinstripe suit cast him in a more businesslike demeanor than Saturday's outfit from the "Sound of Music" costume closet. But the serious image didn't last long: Rising from a side table, Gerbils tripped over one of the 15 microphone cords leading to the dais and, grasping to catch himself, knocked over the chief's water pitcher. With a flash of sparks and a painful popping noise, the amplifier went dead. Behind Gerbils, DeWitt Vanderpol slapped a hand over his eyes.

Gerbils, his eyes popping from his round, nearly hairless head, cleared his throat, gave a solicitous nod to van Dyke's black-veiled widow, standing in an alcove, and spoke into the microphones as if nothing had happened.

"I just wanted to say…I just wanted to tell all of Portland that Pieter van Dyke was not only our inspirational and hardworking colleague, he was our friend," he said in a quavering voice with a slight German accent that came out only when the Oregon-born lawyer was under stress. German was the language in the Gerbils home when Gerhard was a young child and his grandfather lived with them.

"Can you speak up, the mike isn't working!" came a cry from the back row.

Gerbils' eyes darted around the room as if looking for a savior, but no tech-savvy amplifier expert stepped forward. He tried again, with his family heritage asserting itself even more in his speech.

"I chust wanted to say that Pieter was not only our colleague, but our friend," he repeated.

"LOUDER, PLEASE!" came another call from the back.

"PIETER WAS NOT CHUST A COLLEAGUE, HE VAS OUR FRIEND!" Gerbils said, turning red and almost shouting now. "He is...that is, he *vas* our friend and colleague, and a high-minded civic hero in der community!"

As if surprised at his own vehemence, Gerbils paused and cocked his head, then continued, articulating more carefully now.

"We are shocked at the heinous crime that has taken this God-fearing, public-spirited leader from our midst, and while my friend DeWitt Vanderpol and I will soldier bravely on in Pieter's tradition, we vow to work within the legal community to ensure that no effort is spared to bring to justice whomever is responsible!" Now he was hitting his stride, the round little man thought to himself.

"And let me just say, that if that determination and vigilance leads to the godless pagans to whom our police chief refers, I say this: BRING. ZEM. ON!"

A stunned hush filled the room.

At the back, leaning in an unlit corner where they seemed to have been corralled by snaking TV cables, Nate Darrow shook his head and muttered into Harry Harrington's ear, "Oh, goody, sounds like we're paying a social call on the tie-dye terrorists of Sauvie Island."

Chapter Seven

With the bookmobile sidelined until a police forensics team finished gathering evidence, Hester reported Wednesday morning to a temporary reassignment at Portland's Grand Central Library, downtown on Tenth Avenue.

She'd been instructed to divide her time over the next few days between two assignments: taking inventory of the library's prized McLoughlin Collection, eclectic holdings of art and artifacts donated over many decades by Portland's wealthiest benefactors, and filling in for vacation absences on Reference Line, the library's ask-us-anything telephone information service.

While the McLoughlin assignment spoke of the administration's high regard for her competence, the Reference Line gig was more Hester's idea of fun. The eight-member "Answer Crew" was not only smart and quick witted, but their morning ritual of racing in teams to complete the daily New York Times crossword puzzle – the losers bought muffins – appealed to Hester's competitive nature.

She'd subbed there before, so there was little preamble as she plopped down in front of the bank of phones. To perk up her mood, she was wearing the lavender sundress with hand-stitching by her aunt that she wore only in warm weather.

"Hester! What's a four-letter word starting with 'g' for 'trivia-loving oaf in eyeglasses,'" called out young Sean Archer, whose amazing knowledge of minutiae made him the unchallenged Reference Line whiz kid, a proud status reflected in a glint in his eye, easily seen even through his horn-rimmed spectacles.

"That would be 'geek,' Sean," Hester cooed, with a pat on the curly blond head of her favorite crossword partner.

"So sorry about what happened with you guys and the bookmobile, Hester!" commiserated Holly Fontana, another phone specialist, whose matronly figure was a testimonial to the wonderful cookies she baked and often shared with her cohorts. "Why on earth would anyone do that to Pieter?"

Her use of van Dyke's first name wasn't uncommon; his social whirl brought him in contact with people of every stratum, even if just for a holiday-time "meet and greet" in the library lobby. Many in Grand Central felt as if they'd lost a friend.

"Oh, goodness, I can't begin to guess," Hester responded, puffing out her cheeks in bewilderment over the previous day's events. "Some people are hinting at a Rajneeshee connection, but that sounds pretty loony, doesn't it? I think those poisoned salad bars made our police chief a little paranoid."

Phones started ringing then, precluding further discussion. Hester soon found herself paging through almanacs in search of the weight of an average housefly. You never knew what callers would ask, which is why Reference Line was rarely boring.

"As long as they don't ask how many angels can dance on the head of a pin, we're happy," Sean confided in her at lunch break. "As often as not, we're probably just settling somebody's bar bet."

After lunch, Hester climbed the grandly curving marble staircase that ascended from the lobby, past stone columns reaching four stories high to a gilded ceiling, and made her way to the McLoughlin Room.

By 3 p.m. her eyes were already crossing as she carefully checked off items on a spreadsheet. The paintings were easy to account for: Big 19th-century Rubenesque nudes by a Dutch painter who might have been Pieter van Dyke's great uncle crowded the walls. If a painting was missing, the bare spot on the wall would be a giveaway.

But the scores of other artifacts took more attention. Until she'd gone through a big album of them, Hester had never heard of first-day covers, fine-stationery mailing envelopes embossed with historical illustrations related to the subject of a new postage stamp that was affixed to the envelope and custom-canceled on the first day the stamp was issued. The McLoughlin Collection included what was apparently a valuable trove of them, donated – incidentally – by Pieter Van Dyke's father.

"So how's it going, Miss McGarrigle?" asked Dabney Pensler, the McLoughlin Collection archivist, striding in as Hester was finishing her day and pulling off a sweater she'd brought to wear in these over-air-conditioned cloisters.

A tall and high-strung man who reminded Hester of Ichabod Crane, Pensler was the only real human being she'd ever met who actually wore pince nez, through which he delighted in peering at you down his beaklike nose. Rarely did anyone introduced to him go five minutes before they'd learned not only that he was a member of Mensa, but that he was only in Portland "on special loan" from the prestigious Martinbury Institute in Philadelphia. His "special loan" was stretching on toward 15 years now.

"Oh, Dabney. It's a big job, isn't it?" Hester replied, stacking her sheets of work into a big manila envelope.

"Oh, yes, it's a tremendous responsibility," he said, preening at his thick, gray hair, swept back in a Paul Revere pony tail.

"I'm glad you stopped by, because I did find one problem, and it's kind of a big one," Hester continued. "All I found was an empty box for the Charbonneau pistol replica. Do you know anything about that?"

The lanky man's eyebrows rose toward the ceiling and his pince nez fell from his nose and swung like a pendulum on a burgundy sateen ribbon that circled his collar.

"The Charbonneau? Missing? What on earth do you mean?"

"Well, I mean it's not there. There's a nice archival box with all the detailed labels and the provenance record, but nothing inside but velvet wrappings. It appears from the paperwork that we loaned it to Fort Vancouver for a special event in May and apparently it was never returned."

The rosewood-handled pistol with steel barrel and handsome brass fittings was an exact copy of the 1801 French flintlock cavalry pistol carried on the Lewis and Clark expedition by French trapper and guide Toussaint Charbonneau. The replica was made in 1905 for the

McLoughlin family by the same French gunsmithery as the original, to help mark the 100th anniversary of the famous Corps of Discovery exploration. Even as a replica, it was worth thousands for its authenticity and antiquity.

Hester had never seen a man wring his hands as vigorously, in true praying mantis style.

"Well, they must still have it!" Pensler croaked. "We must call them immediately! I'm sure the National Park Service has taken proper care with it, but it was to be returned within a week. This is inexcusable!"

"Dabney, I've already left an urgent message for their curator to get back to me," Hester said in her most soothing voice. "And it happens I'm going up there tomorrow on another errand. My colleague Ethel Pimala is there helping with a re-enactment and we're meeting for lunch – remember I told you I'd just be in for the afternoon? So I'll be sure to track down the pistol and escort it back here personally."

Pensler pulled out a linen handkerchief monogrammed with "DP" in old English letters and mopped the dripping sweat from his forehead. With Hester's calming words he quickly composed himself.

"Well, that will be fine then." He sniffed, replaced his pince nez, and peered down his nose at Hester. "You'll keep me informed?"

"Of course. I'll talk to you tomorrow."

Hester sighed as the storklike man strode through the room's carved oak doors.

"My, I've earned my little paycheck today," she whispered as she gathered her purse and followed him out.

Chapter Eight

Harry Harrington was buck naked except for a strategically draped beach towel that he wore like Superman's cape to cover his backside and a beach ball he carried in front of him.

Walking behind him, Nate Darrow, who refused to remove his clothing, noticed a butterfly-shaped birthmark on his colleague's bony right shoulder as the two detectives wound their way on a dusty trail past snowberries and beneath mossy cottonwoods toward Collins Beach, Sauvie Island's famed nude sunning spot. It was such an institution that there was even an official county sign out by the road informing the public that the beach was clothing-optional.

They'd been directed here after stopping up the road at Downward Dog Farm only to be told that the farm's Spiritual Leader, Ma Anand Martha, was spending the day "renewing her oneness with the Sun God, Ra." The late-spring heat had returned to northern Oregon.

"I've read about these people, and you can't expect them to cooperate unless you're on the same spiritual plane, and that means getting bare," the balding, fifty-something Harrington had lectured Darrow at their parked car as he stripped down with what Nate found to be discomfiting zeal. Nate breathed a small sigh of relief when Harry pulled his modesty-ensuring beach accessories from the car's trunk.

"OK, Harry, you can take the lead on this interview, and I wish you luck, but I'm keeping my pants on," Darrow told him. "I don't mind skinny dipping now and then, but the whole idea of these nudists who go on picnics, munch fried chicken, play Twister and pretend that everything is perfectly normal while way too many things are hanging out in the breeze, just kind of gives me the heebie-jeebies."

"Well, Nate, my friend, the missus and I are no naturists, but she has a crazy aunt down in Bandon who's always talked up this sort of thing,"

Harrington replied, pushing his perennially slipping eyeglasses up with one hand and then patting his careful comb-over back into place, while the other hand carefully grasped the multicolored beach ball to his waist as they walked.

"She says baring your soul to the universe is the spiritual equivalent of a high colonic. She sent my wife's cousin to this crazy school that always sounded to me like that place Auntie Mame sent little Patrick Dennis, you know? Where they all swam like salmon going upstream to spawn? Did you ever see that movie?"

It didn't take long to find Ma Anand Martha on the sandy Columbia River beach. She and a group of four deeply tanned followers were the only beachgoers with a tie-dyed kite, soaring in the breeze above them, tethered to the ground by a string of Tibetan prayer flags.

Nate hung back near the tree line, hands in pockets, and watched as Harry introduced himself and flashed his badge, which he had pinned to his beach towel. As he spoke, Ma Anand Martha, a freckled brunette whose demeanor was more La Jolla than Lhasa, provocatively rubbed baby oil on her breasts. Nate heard Harry choke three times during their exchange of words, muffled by a soft breeze blowing down the river.

"Let's just hope he doesn't need his gun," Darrow thought to himself, watching idly as a heavily laden inbound freighter with "TOYOTA" in giant letters across its topsides pushed aside a high bow wave as it trundled 50 yards from shore on its way to the Port of Portland.

But the conversation was surprisingly calm and brief. After a few minutes Harrington pulled out a ballpoint pen – from where? Darrow wondered – and jotted something down on his beach ball.

"They say they have an airtight alibi," Harry told Nate as they kicked up a small dust cloud from the dry path on their walk back to the car. "The night van Dyke was killed all 10 members of their group were up all night long in their barn because their favorite horse was giving birth. They say the local veterinarian can vouch for them."

Twenty-five minutes later, with Harrington again attired in the blue-and-white striped seersucker suit he favored in warm weather, they were in the log-cabin-style Sauvie Island Animal Clinic watching Dr. Nigel

Hartley give a mewling tabby kitten its first vaccinations. Hartley, who sounded like a transplant from New Zealand or Australia, was confirming the Rajneeshees' story.

"Yes, mates, I was there all night with them, from about 8 p.m. until almost bloody 6 in the morning," said the plaid-shirted, mutton-chopped vet, shaking his shaggy brown locks at the memory. "Those folks are good clients and they care about their animals, but crikey, they almost drove me round the twist that night. It was Rainbow, their favorite miniature horse. They got her with the idea of breeding and selling the offspring – you'd be amazed what you can get for these novelty breeds. But they're so loopy over their animals I don't think they'll ever give one up."

He paused while he took the kitten back to a Dutch door and handed it over to its waiting owner, a shyly smiling 8-year-old girl from a nearby farmhouse.

"There you go, little Madeline, now be sure Squeaker gets a bowl of cream as a treat when you get her home," the kindly vet told her, then turned back to Darrow and continued.

"Anyway, they were there all night chanting and burning incense," Hartley continued as he washed his hands over a basin next to the door. "And I know it was all of them because I kept trying to suggest that we didn't *need* 10 people to assist and maybe some of them should get some sleep, but they wouldn't hear of it.

"So it turned out the little mare was bursting with twin foals in a bad presentation and I had to do a C-section, and I tell you it took about two hours of palavering to convince them it was necessary and that just giving her a beet-juice enema wouldn't solve the problem!"

Hartley agreed that he would sign a sworn statement if necessary, and Nate and Harry stepped back out into the bright sunshine, breathing deeply of the interesting mix of aromas on the breeze: floral scents from a neighboring nursery and earthy manure from a dairy farm.

As Harrington guided the Caprice back across the narrow old steel-girder bridge over Multnomah Channel, a Willamette River offshoot that separated the island from the mainland, Darrow drummed his fingers on the dashboard and frowned in thought.

"Harry, I don't want to know what the captain is going to say when he hears that we struck out with the Rajneeshees, and I hate to think what he's going to tell the chief," Darrow said, sucking on his teeth.

Harrington, the veteran of many bosses and several chiefs, seemed to be taking it in stride.

"You just tell the truth, Nate," he said, twirling the steering wheel to merge onto Highway 30 back toward the city. "The quick arrest the chief promised the public was foiled by a bunch of prayer-flag waving nudists chanting over a miniature horse named Rainbow."

Darrow rubbed his temples and squeezed his eyes shut. "Yeah, that's what I was afraid you were going to say."

He flinched when a furious beeping sounded from his jacket. Fumbling and scrambling to find his new cellular phone, something all Portland detectives had been issued two weeks earlier, Darrow finally fished the phone from his pocket, raised its little antenna, peered at it long enough to pick out the "answer" button and held it to his ear. "Hello! Nate Darrow."

Poking an index finger into his other ear in an effort to hear, Darrow listened silently, then said, *"Really?"* Muttering thanks he punched the button to hang up. As he pushed the antenna down he gave a low whistle.

"Well, this case just gets weirder," he said with a glance at Harrington.

"What! Tell me."

"That was Jerry Lorente at the medical examiner's, fresh from the autopsy, where he recovered the slug that killed van Dyke. It had apparently lodged against his spine."

"Yeah, and what's so interesting that he had to call you on that dad-blamed high-tech gizmo?" Harrington wheedled, waggling his shaggy eyebrows like a shrimp Darrow had seen in a tank at Jake's Famous Crawfish, one of his favorite Portland restaurants. Nate had quickly discovered the fun of keeping Harry in suspense.

"Well, it wasn't your garden variety .38 or .22," Darrow added, pausing to chew on a thumbnail.

"Yeah, AND?" Now Harry was turning the same red as that shrimp.

"Well, according to Jerry, it looks a lot like – well, a lot like a musket ball."

Chapter Nine

Thursday, June 13

S niffing at the faint odor of disinfectant hanging in the assistant ME's office at 8:30 the next morning, Darrow sat across a cluttered desk from a man in green scrubs who munched a toasted "everything" bagel, talking with his mouth half-full and spraying poppy seeds and fragments of garlic as he spoke.

"First time I've seen anything like it," said Jerry Lorente, a fair-skinned, dark-haired Hispanic who periodically reached up with thumb and forefinger to absently pluck at his mustache as he spoke. "But I did a little research and what we have is a lead ball such as was commonly used in firearms of the early to mid-19th century."

Lorente used a pair of tongs to pull the slightly misshapen ball from a zip-lock evidence bag and drop it with a loud "plunk" in a metal tray for Darrow's inspection.

Darrow tugged off his gray corduroy sport coat as the room's fuggy atmosphere started to make his head swim.

"So," he shrugged, in bewilderment, "Who even *has* guns like that around Portland, Oregon, in 1996?"

"Hey, I know who!" erupted a voice from the room's open doorway.

Both men's heads swiveled. Against the doorjamb leaned Gavin Peacock, the office's resident know-it-all, in scrubs flecked liberally with something brown and yellowish that Darrow didn't want to analyze too closely.

Nate had encountered him in the line of duty a couple times and couldn't decide which was more off-putting: Peacock's high-pitched, raspy voice or his waggling, skunk-striped beard, cut in the Lincoln style to frame his weak chin but with no mustache. It worked on Honest Abe,

but smacked of pretension at the end of the 20th century, Nate thought
privately.

"OK, spill," Darrow responded as Peacock smirked.

"I have a cousin who's into historical re-enactments, you know, of
Civil War battles and all that sort of thing, and they have a whole group
over at Fort Vancouver – the 'First Oregon Volunteer Infantry' – that does
demonstrations with muskets and flintlocks and that sort of gun," Peacock
said. "I'll bet you might find out exactly what fired that ball if you go talk
to folks at the national historic site."

Darrow listened thoughtfully, realizing this was the first time
Peacock had actually said something useful within his hearing.

Slapping his thigh, Darrow flung his jacket over his sweat-stained
shirt back and rose without delay. "That, my skunk-bearded friend, is a
great idea."

❖

Thirty minutes later Darrow and Harry Harrington were sitting in
stopped traffic on the Interstate Bridge at the north edge of Portland as
they watched the tower of a Tidewater Barge Co. tug glide beneath the
raised drawbridge.

The tug was pushing a barge filled with frozen French fries
downriver to Portland after making the 300-mile trip from Lewiston,
Idaho. But all Nate and Harry knew was that it was holding them up.

"I swear to God, they must have a special scanner set up that sees
me coming, because this bridge goes up *every* darn time I try to cross over
to Washington," Harrington complained.

Darrow, having grown numb to Harry's protestations about traffic
conspiracies, let his eyes wander to the car stopped in the lane next to
them: a blue Civic hatchback with "WASH ME" written in the dust on its
fender. Beyond, in the far distance, the perfectly conical snowy peak of
Mount Hood rose over the river.

As his eyes idly wandered over the next car the driver suddenly turned and looked straight into his eyes. Darrow glanced away in embarrassment.

Then he turned back.

He and the blue-eyed driver of the next car simultaneously rolled down their windows.

"Hester!"

"Nate!"

"We run into each other in the weirdest places," Darrow said to his favorite librarian. "Hey, where you heading?"

"Oh, Pim had a thing in Vancouver this morning and we're meeting for lunch – it's her birthday!" Hester called across the traffic line.

At that moment the bridge deck finished lowering and the gates went up, so Harry pulled forward and Darrow waved to Hester and closed his window.

The Caprice zoomed ahead the last 500 feet to Washington soil, and Harry took the signed exit toward Fort Vancouver National Historic Site.

Founded in 1824, Fort Vancouver was one of the first outposts of European settlers in this corner of the continent. Originally it was a Hudson's Bay Co. fur-trading post. Later it doubled as a military installation for the U.S. Army, with early officers including Ulysses S. Grant and other famous names. Now it was run by the National Park Service, with an authentic replica of the original wooden fort, complete with blacksmith shop, fur warehouse and a chief factor's house with cannons out front.

Harry steered the Caprice around a traffic circle and along Officers Row, a stately line of restored, maple-shaded officer homes – now subdivided into ritzy rental townhouses – and hung a right on a winding drive to cross grassy parade grounds to the fort.

Darrow and Harrington were conferring at the log-built gatehouse with a park ranger, whose long gray braids hung down on both sides of her Smokey Bear hat, when who should walk up the gravel path from the parking lot but Hester McGarrigle.

Today, Hester was outfitted for the weather in olive-colored slacks and a cream-colored cotton blouse emblazoned with a bamboo print. She carried a broad-brimmed straw hat, part of a large hat collection that she loved in concept but could rarely stand to wear on the grounds that hats were too claustrophobic.

The ranger continued to talk as Darrow pantomimed his surprise and waved hello to Hester, who stopped and hovered within hearing distance.

"The guy you really need to talk to is our head curator, John Vouri, he's the historical firearms expert here," the ranger said in a gravelly voice, taking off her hat to fan herself on the hot day. "But I'm afraid he's on family leave in Ohio and won't be back for a few more days. I don't really have anyone else on staff who can talk much about that sort of thing, but John's a wizard on that stuff."

"Oh, dear, that's who I'd hoped to see as well," Hester spoke up, drawing the others' attention. "But Detective Darrow, why are you here?"

Darrow caught a warning glance and a throat-clearing from Harrington, to whom he gave a perfunctory, slightly annoyed nod of reassurance before responding. "Uh, it's part of an investigation." The obvious message-left-unsaid: "I can't talk to you about it."

Darrow and Hester had a personal history that was a poorly kept secret among a few of his colleagues. That it had happened when she was a primary witness in a case he was working, potentially risking his job had the brass found out, had created some awkwardness between them. The fling had been short-lived, though the attraction still smoldered.

Hester caught the implication. She looked at him quizzically for a moment.

"Well, you might not be able to talk about it, but I can talk about why *I'm* here, and frankly it doesn't hurt for the police to hear," she forged on.

Now she had their full attention. Hester peered at the nameplate on the ranger's breast pocket.

"Ranger McPhee, I work for the Portland City Library and today I represent the McLoughlin Collection, our collection of art and artifacts named, as you probably know, for your fort's original chief factor, John McLoughlin."

Ranger McPhee's braids danced as she nodded.

"And at Memorial Day, for one of your re-enactments, we loaned you folks a valuable replica of a historical French flintlock pistol, what we call the Charbonneau pistol," Hester continued. "It was to be returned within a few days, but we discovered yesterday that it's not where it should be, so we're wondering if there was some delay in getting it back from you folks, perhaps?"

As she spoke, Darrow and Harrington exchanged meaningful glances and Nate saw that Harry's eyebrows were starting to do the shrimp thing again.

Now concern clouded Ranger McPhee's age-crinkled face.

"Boy, I wish I could help you there. I can take a look around John's office but I don't have keys to his gun lockup. I'm afraid he left in rather a hurry right after the Memorial Day events – his father had a heart attack. And sadly the old man died a week later, so John stayed on for the funeral and is attending to some estate matters before he returns."

Hester's hand flew up to cover her mouth.

"I could maybe get him on the phone if you need," Ranger McPhee concluded.

"Oh, no, no – I'm sorry to hear of his circumstances, let's not bother the poor man," Hester said. "I expect it's probably in a safe place and we'll get it back when he returns. I think I can placate our curator with that."

"Ahem," Darrow interjected. "This, uh, pistol you're talking about…Would it by any chance shoot something that looks like a musket ball?"

Hester appeared dumbfounded by the question. "I really have no idea, but why on earth are you asking?"

But Ranger McPhee spoke up in response to Nate's question.

"If it's something we were using in our re-enactments, then, yes, it would most likely shoot a standard lead ball like you'd see used in muskets from the early 19th century, I can tell you that much," she said.

"In fact, they were just using firearms like that in a re-enactment rehearsal here earlier this morning. Unfortunately, I saw the volunteer in charge of that part of the program drive out of here about 20 minutes ago or you could have picked *his* brain."

Darrow pinched his lip in thought. As he looked out across the fort, he saw Ethel Pimala approaching from the direction of the fort's vegetable garden. She wore one of her garish Hawaiian shirts and directed a beaming smile toward Hester.

"Hester, did you say you were going to have lunch with Pim?" Darrow asked. "I wonder if I could crash your party and join you?"

"Why – sure," Hester stammered.

Harrington cast a stern eye at Darrow. "Nate, we really need to get back – "

"It's OK, I'll get a ride back to town with Hester," he consoled Harry, then cocking a questioning eyebrow at the intrepid librarian. "That OK with you?"

Hester shrugged in confusion. "I don't see why not. The more the merrier."

Chapter Ten

The Wiener Dog Restaurant was something of an institution along Interstate 5 at Jantzen Beach, the first bit of land after southbound motorists crossed the Columbia River bridge from Washington to Oregon. The restaurant's giant freeway-side sign with a smiling neon dachshund was a delightful bit of 1960s kitsch, Hester thought. She considered it a good omen whenever the sign was switched on so that the tail wagged madly as she drove past.

It was the perfect place for a birthday lunch for Pim, whose mustard-spotted collection of Aloha shirts offered mute testimony of her appreciation for anything hot-dog-like.

"This place grinds their own meats *and* bakes the poppy-seed kaiser rolls fresh every morning, and that seedy German mustard in the crockery pot on every table is flown in straight from the old country," Pim told Hester and Nate as they were seated in a red vinyl corner banquette by a bustling little man in brown jodhpurs, an immaculate white shirt and skinny black tie.

"Thank you, Herr Commandant," Darrow muttered under his breath, feeling for a moment that the man looked familiar but dismissing it with the thought that he'd watched too much "Hogan's Heroes" as a kid.

"So, Pim how did your practice go?" Hester asked after the host had poured a round of Pim's favorite German wine, Blue Nun, and they had toasted her birthday.

Turning to Darrow, Hester interjected, "Pim is going to lead one of the fort's Fourth of July re-enactments. It's the first time they're staging something that gives recognition to the large workforce of Hawaiians who did much of the farming and hard labor that kept this frontier outpost running back when the only Portland anybody around here had heard of was in Maine. The old square-rigger supply ships coming around the Horn tended to swing out as far as Hawaii before catching a favorable wind to the Pacific Northwest."

Darrow listened attentively. He sometimes teased Hester when she got "all school marm-ish," but he also found it charming.

In answer to Hester's query, Pim puffed out her coffee-colored cheeks like a squirrel with a mouthful of walnuts.

"Well, we might just have to can the whole pandanus weaving demo – I *told* Nancy Mitchell rhododendron leaves would be a crappy substitute!" the little woman groaned. "But the dancing is coming along," she said, turning to Darrow. "We got the pep squad gals from Hudson's Bay High across the river there to come up with sort of an Indian hula, combining Hawaiian dance with some of the native dances from the local Chinook tribes, who provided most of the wives for the men at the fort – even the ones who had other wives back East somewhere." She chortled and gave the detective a bawdy wink.

Hester chimed in with a prim smile. "It's true, I was reading about it in one of the McLoughlin Collection histories. The soldiers called them their 'country wives.' "

Darrow took a sip of the wine and winced. "Oh, that's good and sweet. I've got this molar that's reacting badly to sugary things."

After a moment with his face screwed up, Darrow blinked his eyes three times fast, then straightened out and directed a question to Pim.

"So – Ranger McPhee said there was a musket demonstration as part of your gig this morning?"

Pim's brown eyes lit up.

"Yeah, I think that will be one of the more popular things, they're doing a target practice with papayas on top of fence posts. Some of the Kanaka folk – that's what they called them – actually had brought along seeds and tried to grow them, though I don't know how much success they had," Pim enthused, casually pushing her empty wineglass toward Darrow. He obliged by refilling it from a carafe. After hoisting the glass and slurping another mouthful, she continued.

"And what is really cool is that the guy who's leading the shooting demonstration is my friend Pomp Charbonneau. He says he's something like the great, great, great, great grandson of one of the guides on the Lewis and Clark expedition! The one who was married to Sacajawea!"

She sat back with a triumphant grin. Hester smiled in appreciation, and privately appreciated watching Darrow arch his luxuriant eyebrows. Pim was obviously enjoying her day in the spotlight. The bookmobile driver didn't pause long.

"Pomp is such a practical joker. You know what he did today? Hester, you remember that awful raccoon hat he wore in the parade?"

Hester shuddered and nodded.

"Well he shows up today for our practice and we all see that he's wearing that awful hat again. So we just try to ignore it, until halfway into the shooting practice, see, he suddenly reaches into the pocket of his buckskin coat, pulls out a tin of sardines, cracks it open and starts feeding them to his hat!"

Quizzical looks from Hester and Nate brought a huge laugh from Pim, who eagerly continued.

"It turns out that not only does he have that awful hat, he also has a real, live pet raccoon that he's trained to sit on his head! He calls it Meriwether, just as a poke in the eye to old Lewis, who apparently never liked the original Charbonneau!"

Satisfied that her anecdote had properly mystified them, she returned to the subject of the shooting demonstration.

"Oh, and what visitors are really going to love – it's not just with muskets. Pomp has this classic French flintlock pistol that actually was used by his great-great-granddaddy-whatever when he was with the Corps of Discovery," Pim added, mispronouncing "Corps" like "corpse," as if talking about a dead body.

Darrow, whose earlier eyebrow arching was mostly polite pretense, had been absently eyeing the jodhpur-clad maitre d', whose lack of customers had led him to fuss over table settings. The fussing had now evolved into maniacal glass polishing two tables away from them, his back turned.

But at Pim's latest statement Darrow sat up straight and tuned into what she'd said.

"What? You say he has an old flintlock pistol? That shoots lead balls?"

Pim reveled in the interest, taking a long sip of the tooth-curlingly sweet riesling before responding.

"Sure, it's pretty much the same kind of ammo they use in the muskets. Why are you so interested, Inspector?"

Darrow hesitated just a moment before his intuition told him this was a time to share a confidence.

"It turns out that some kind of musket-ball gun might have been involved in Pieter van Dyke's murder," he said, "and it would make sense that it was a pistol, in the circumstances."

As a look of consternation crossed Pim's face, Darrow quickly continued.

"Don't get me wrong, I'm not suggesting your friend had anything to do with it, but if he knows a lot about guns like that I'm thinking he might help me learn more about what we're looking for. Does he live nearby?"

Pim squinted at him, then seemed satisfied with his response.

"Well, actually he lives out in the wine country, out toward McMinnville. Being a Frenchie, he's started making wine in his barn, and it's almost as good as this!" she said, holding aloft her glass of Blue Nun.

Before Darrow could ask more, the maitre d' was suddenly clearing his throat behind him, making Nate jump.

"So, what can I bring you folks for lunch?" he asked.

After they all agreed on the daily special of bratwurst on kaiser rolls with sides of German potato salad and house-made sauerkraut, their host retreated to the kitchen.

"Goodness, the poor man has to do everything here, I guess," Hester observed sympathetically, trying to steer the birthday conversation away from murder. "This place used to be so popular. I wonder if they're doing OK?"

"You know, it's just not fair how the health crazies have given hot dogs and sausages a bad rap lately," Pim responded, speaking with the irresistible charm of a fanatic. "There used to be five Wiener Dogs around

Portland, all with happy wagging signs, and since everybody started eating sushi, one by one the Wieners have shut down so now there's just this original one. And look, we're the only people here at lunchtime. Can you believe that?"

"It's a…a crying shame when favorite old places fall on hard times," Hester commiserated.

"It's been so hard on Mr. Gerbils, I tell you," Pim said in a whisper, nodding toward their host, who was returning from the kitchen.

Darrow stopped wadding up paper balls from a drinking-straw wrapper and looked up.

"Did you say 'Gerbils'?" He turned and cast a sharp look at the restaurateur, now furiously dusting a wall of framed black-and-white photos showing what appeared to be smiling celebrities posing as they took bites from Wiener Dog hot dogs. (Was that really John Wayne?) Recognition dawned in Darrow's eyes.

"I thought he was a lawyer!" Darrow hissed, turning back to his dining companions.

"Oh, he is!" Pim beamed, happy for possessing a bit of knowledge that put the detective at a disadvantage. She paused to sip some wine.

"And – ? Why's he here shoveling bratwurst?" Darrow whispered with impatience.

"Well, Inspector, this was the Gerbils family's first endeavor when they came to America – it started with a mule-drawn lunch wagon that served hot dogs to the shipyard workers who built all them WWII Liberty ships on the banks of the Columbia," Pim explained smugly. "The family got out of Krautland just ahead of Hitler's goosesteppers."

"Pim!" Hester shushed her, turning pink at her co-worker's plain language.

"And the son who has the business now did become a lawyer, in the same firm as Pieter van Dyke, as you probably know," Pim forged on. "But he only ever did that to pay the bills. His first love is The Wiener Dog. I seen him here every time I've come."

Darrow's mind reeled as they ate their lunch. Had Gerbils overheard his less-than-discreet comments about van Dyke's murder? He didn't want to seem insensitive. Nor, when it came to it, did he need his captain hearing about this from an indignant colleague of the victim.

His musings were interrupted only by "yums" and "mmms" as his companions chomped their hot dogs, punctuated by Pim's happy squeal as she took a big bite and her bratwurst sprayed grease across her Aloha shirt, this one decorated with ukulele-playing surfers riding waves at Waikiki.

"You know they're good when that happens," she crowed.

Darrow insisted on paying, and when the restaurateur returned his credit card with the slip to sign, he again stopped and cleared his throat. Darrow looked up.

"Excuse me for interrupting, but – it is Detective Darrow, isn't it? I thought I might have recognized you from the news reports."

"Oh, yes, Mr. Gerbils, hello. I didn't recognize you at first…"

"Of course. It is a very different context from my law office, but the restaurant is my first love." Gerbils' eyes, seemingly too small for his head, darted nervously as he gave a soapy grin. "I hope your lunch pleased you?"

Darrow smiled and nodded. The rotund man hesitated, then continued in a serious vein.

"If you'll forgive me, I just want to say that I hope the police remember that Pieter van Dyke had a long and varied law career, as did his father and grandfather, and many men went to prison or paid other prices when they were on the losing side against the van Dykes. People make enemies in our profession."

He stood silently, clicking his ballpoint pen, then concluded.

"If you're thinking of ruling out the Rajneeshees, Mr. Darrow, I hope you'll look at anybody who has gotten out of prison recently – anybody who might have been there because of Pieter van Dyke or his family!"

Chapter Eleven

As they stopped to drop Pim at the bookmobile barn in Northeast Portland, Darrow groaned as he unfolded his 6-foot-2 frame from the back seat of Hester's well-traveled two-door Civic. He had insisted that the "birthday girl" take the roomier front seat, regretting it the moment Pim hopped in and slid the seat all the way back, putting Darrow's knees under his chin.

"Do you know you have eight rolls of wide, clear tape rolling around the floor of the car back there?" he asked Hester as he settled into the front seat.

"Oh. That's where it keeps disappearing to," she said with a thoughtful look. "You're in a librarian's car, sir, and that is the librarian's friend – book tape. It's used for mending paperback covers and that sort of thing. Sort of our version of duct tape. That stuff would mend the Eiffel Tower if it ever broke. I'm rarely without it."

His feet still tingled with the feeling returning to them as Hester guided the car toward the police headquarters.

They rode silently for several blocks, but as Hester began to turn toward the Burnside Bridge, beneath the giant White Stag Sportswear sign with its iconic leaping deer outlined in white neon, they both started to speak at the same moment.

"Say, Nate – "

"Hester – "

Both grinned with a little embarrassment. "You first," Darrow interjected.

Hester smiled and nodded thanks.

"I didn't know if I should say anything in front of Pim, but that Charbonneau friend of hers – His ancestor's pistol she was talking about..." Hester hesitated.

"Yes?" Darrow goaded her, fidgeting with some book tape that had rolled forward from beneath his seat.

"The pistol missing from the McLoughlin Collection was a copy of that pistol," Hester blurted.

Darrow's response was cut off by a shrill beeping from his sport coat. "Oh, that damn thing again," Nate cursed as he slapped at various pockets to find the cellphone. Finally he fished it from an inside breast pocket.

"Yeah, Harry, I'm almost back to the office, what's up?" Darrow responded after the initial greeting.

Hester heard a muted squawking from the earpiece and watched Darrow's brow knit. "No shit, Sherlock?" he asked his colleague after a few moments. "Harry, hang in there, I'll be there in five."

Pocketing the phone, Darrow took a deep breath and clicked his teeth together a few times before explaining to Hester.

"Well, a fisherman on the creek at the edge of Forest Park spotted something that had caught in the old grating where the stream disappears under the Thurman overpass – it must have washed up after our little thunderstorm last night," he said. "And it appears we not only may have found the gun that killed van Dyke, but from the French manufacturer's name on it and the little 'Portland City Library' metal sticker on the bottom of the grip, I'm betting it's your missing pistol."

Hester's mouth hung open. "Oh, my lord."

A thought dawned on Darrow and he pulled out his cellphone again.

"Maybe I can make good use of this gadget for once," he announced, peering at a list of phone numbers that had been preprogrammed into the phone when he got it. Finally finding what he sought, he hesitantly punched three buttons in succession, and when an answer came, he spoke briskly.

"Yeah, Konnie, it's Nate Darrow. I wonder if you could get me everything you can find on a guy named Charbonneau. First name of Pomp – P-O-M-P, as far as I know, probably a nickname but that's all I have. And I'm definitely looking for an address and phone if you can find it."

As he pocketed the phone again, Hester's probing look loosened his tongue.

"Look, I'm still not saying we have anything on Pim's friend, but there are a few too many coincidences here and his name keeps popping up," Darrow explained.

"Goodness, I don't think you're ever going to be Pim's favorite," Hester said ruefully.

Darrow gave an audible sigh. "Thanks for the ride, I'll tell him she says hi," he finished, as he jumped out of the car in front of the Portland Police Bureau.

Chapter Twelve

B ack at Grand Central Library that afternoon, the hands on Hester's old Timex said 3:45. For 15 minutes she'd been contemplating a break to dash across the street to Callahan's Confections for a $2 bag of dark chocolate-covered licorice.

But for the past five minutes she'd also been contemplating the ample nude figures in the paintings on the wall opposite her in the McLoughlin Collection gallery.

Peering in concentration at the oil just opposite her, Hester raised one elbow behind her head, pointed her chin skyward and draped a leg over the corner of her old walnut desk in emulation of the 18th-century model's pose.

"My, you could have put the 'hip' in hippo, my dear," she scoffed under her breath, sitting back into her chair. Gritting her teeth, she dug into her purse for the wax-paper bag of celery sticks she'd brought from home.

The healthful snack was cold comfort after the earlier drama of calming Dabney Pensler's nervous fit over the idea that the library's pistol may have been involved in van Dyke's murder. Hester wished she'd at least filled the celery sticks with peanut butter.

Just as she was turning back to the inventory list from which she'd been slowly ticking off items for the past two hours, the phone on her desk jangled.

"Hester, it's Holly Fontana up in the Rotunda – I'm the designated minder for the Corps of Discovery Exhibit this afternoon," came a frantic voice when Hester picked up. "Someone said Dabney went home with another of his stress attacks, but we need someone from the McLoughlin Collection up here *right away*."

Hester stopped in the middle of reaching for another celery stick. "Well, I'm just the pinch-hitter this week, Holly, can't it wait?"

"No, I don't think it can – Hester, I'm sorry, but we have a patron who insists we have a blatant counterfeit in our exhibit!"

❖

"It's a fake! It's a laughable fake, and I can't believe the library would fall for this!"

The hysterical words echoed beneath the vintage leaded-glass domed skylight at the top of Grand Central as the elevator door shuddered open and Hester stepped out.

Dodging a small crowd of curious onlookers that included an overexcited class of backpack-dragging third graders from Oregon City, she tried to quash a wince as she recognized the speaker as one of her lesser-favorite bookmobile patrons. Eldon Purdy wore a smug sense of entitlement almost as regularly as he wore the slightly crushed and sweat-stained Panama hat that perched now atop his stringy, black hair.

The little man's face was blotchy with emotion as he leaned over a glass case that contained part of the library's display of Lewis and Clark artifacts, keyed to this year's Rose Festival theme. Holly Fontana, whose curly brown tresses ordinarily framed a smiling and welcoming face, huddled next to him in a posture of embarrassment, waggling her fingers to try to quiet his protests.

"Mr. Purdy, what seems to be the problem?" Hester cooed in her most patron-calming voice as she strode across the marble floor.

"Did you people even *look* at this display before you opened it to the public or did you just have trained monkeys put it together?" he blustered.

Hester gave him a frozen smile – a practiced expression that silently said, "Yes, I'm a public servant, but I don't have to respond to insults from annoying little men in stupid hats."

She crossed her arms and tapped her toe silently until he chose to elaborate.

Finally, popeyed, he pointed into the case at a display of first-day covers, some of the McLoughlin Collection's trove donated by Pieter van Dyke's father.

"I made a special trip downtown just to see this – I've been a philatelist all my life, and the Flying Canoe error printing of the Corps of Discovery 150th anniversary issue of 1955 is second in rarity *only* to the famed Inverted Jenny!"

Ceasing her tapping, Hester looked puzzled.

"Oh, for goodness sakes, surely any expert putting together an informative public display of United States postage stamps knows about the Jenny!" Purdy fussed, his liver-purple lips pursing. "It was an early 20th-century stamp showing a World War I biplane but it was accidentally printed with the plane flying upside down. They sell to collectors for hundreds of thousands apiece!"

Hester, remembering her mother's coaching in the days when she wore pigtails, silently counted to 10 before responding.

"Well, Mr. Purdy, I have to excuse myself. You've seen me on the bookmobile so you know I'm not the expert who staged this exhibition, but I assure you that my colleagues pay the greatest attention to scholarly detail."

Swallowing hard, she continued. "Still, even the best scholars are eager to learn more. What is it you've discovered?"

Eagerly seizing his moment of tribute, Purdy brushed strings of hair from his eyes and dug into a pocket of a leather briefcase he carried. He pulled out a magnifying glass large enough to convince Sherlock Holmes that size mattered.

"I brought this because I wanted to savor the details of the Flying Canoe first-day cover on display," he simpered. "But imagine my surprise when I saw this."

He placed the magnifying glass, as large as Hester's palm, on the glass display case above the first-day cover in question. In the envelope's upper right corner was a postage stamp with a cancellation reading "First Day of Issue." On the left half of the envelope, a meticulous engraving showed Meriwether Lewis and William Clark wading through a cattail-edged marsh. Purdy stepped back and waved his hand for Hester to take a look.

From her inventory duty, Hester knew a little about the famous Flying Canoe first-day cover. The postage stamp it bore showed the two famous explorers paddling a canoe at the mouth of the Columbia River. But through a printing error, a few batches of the stamps showed the canoe up in the sky instead of on the river's surface, thus the stamp's nickname.

She brushed her auburn hair behind her shoulder and bent to peer through the magnifying glass.

"I'm sorry, I guess I don't know what to look for, it looks about as I expected – there's the canoe up in the sky!" she said with an appreciative chuckle.

"But don't you see!" Purdy fumed. "Count them!"

"Pardon?"

"How many men are in the canoe?"

"Oh!" Hester looked again. "There are, um, three."

"YES!" The little man raised his arms in the air as if signaling a football touchdown.

Hester looked confused. Purdy saw that she didn't understand.

"Don't you see? The Lewis and Clark stamp of 1955 showed only Lewis and Clark in their canoe. Lewis – and – Clark – and – nobody – else!"

❖

Fifteen minutes later, in a quiet backroom of the McLoughlin Collection, Hester pored over the provenance file for the first-day cover, which she had removed from the display and brought along with her.

The file noted that Vincent van Dyke Jr., Pieter's father and a son of a former governor, had acquired the philatelic treasure in 1955 on the day the stamp was issued in Astoria, Ore., a fishing and one-time fur-trading center at the mouth of the Columbia River. Not far from Astoria, on the edge of a marshy slough seen before only by local Indians, deer, beavers and myriad waterfowl, the Corps of Discovery had spent the long, wet winter of 1805-06 in a tiny fort they had built from scratch.

Vincent Jr. was one of only a few dozen collectors to get out of the post office that day with a first-day cover before an observant 12-year-old complained about the printing mistake and asked for his money back. Sales were then suspended.

Hester was amused: The file even noted that the release of the flawed stamps was blamed in part on lax oversight by the local postmaster, absent from the ceremonies because it was opening day of the local salmon-fishing season at the Columbia River's famed Buoy 10. Her father, an avid angler, talked about Buoy 10 as if it was a religious shrine.

Hester's head swam. Taking a deep breath, she again picked up the magnifying glass she had appropriated from Mr. Purdy with the promise of returning it next time the bookmobile came by his stop at Toshmore Court. Actually, even with that promise, he wouldn't give it up until she made a "citizen's arrest," as if that was something a librarian could do, Hester recalled with a tiny grin.

She held the glass up with one hand. With the other she grasped a glossy black-and-white photograph she'd pulled from the file. It was a photo of Vincent van Dyke's Lewis and Clark Flying Canoe first-day cover. The photo was taken the day it was accepted into the collection of the Portland City Library.

In the photo, the stamp showed two explorers in a canoe.

Shifting the magnifying glass to the envelope she had brought downstairs from the rotunda, she again counted three men in the canoe.

Leaning closer so that her nose almost smudged the magnifier's glass lens, she scrutinized the new figure in the center of the canoe. He seemed to be attired in the buckskin clothing of a fur trapper, regalia familiar to anyone who has studied the period.

But what was that on his head? Some kind of animal skin? Cocking the magnifier at a new angle, she realized it was a raccoon. You could see the stripes. But not just a skin. A whole raccoon.

A little bell rang in the back of Hester's mind.

"Hoo boy, it's been a long day," she groaned, leaving the magnifying glass to rest atop the first-day cover for a moment while she rubbed her weary eyes.

Shaking her head to clear it, she looked back down and something at the edge of the magnifier caught her attention.

She quickly picked up the glass and moved it over the engraved picture on the side of the envelope.

"I'll be dilly damned," Hester breathed, unconsciously repeating an oath she'd heard her mother use from the time Hester was still in rompers.

It wasn't plain to the naked eye, but under the magnifier it was almost hard to miss. Interwoven with the reeds and cattails among which the explorers waded were thin, angled letters. In places an "h" looked like a stalk. A "C" formed the edge of a leaf.

Together the tiny letters, like an artist's signature, spelled "POMP CHARBONNEAU."

Chapter Thirteen

Hester was more than ready to decompress at day's end. Happily, she had plans after work to meet her old friend, Karen White, for a beer at one of Portland's coziest new southside watering holes.

The Blue Heron brewpub was named for the city's beautiful official bird. From the quiet Sellwood neighborhood bluff where the craft brewery nestled among the district's renowned antique shops, herons could often be spied soaring over the nearby Oaks Bottom Wildlife Refuge, at the edge of the Willamette River. The birds' distinctive, gargled "gronk, gronk" call always sounded like someone being garroted, Hester thought. Perfect for Portland, she believed: elegance with an odd twist.

Hester hadn't seen Karen for more than a couple quick coffee breaks in the four months since her old school friend had revealed that she had been leading a secret life under the pen name of Teri June, author of a best-selling series of "tell it like it is" novels for preteen girls. The books had been at the core of a book-banning controversy that involved Sara Duffy, the murdered librarian. The attendant publicity had given a huge boost to Teri June's flagging sales.

"Well, look at you! Things must be going better!" Hester exclaimed as she spotted Karen at a corner table beneath raw oak beams, slowly whirling ceiling fans, and low-hanging light fixtures fashioned from ... were those pony kegs?

Karen was wearing a flamboyant linen sheath dress festooned with giant sunflowers that shouted "Provence." The tight, shapeless garments were the kind of thing often seen on wealthy, overly tanned and whippet-thin older women. On short, well-padded Karen, it reminded Hester of one of her nana's stuffed rigatonis.

Karen jumped up and the two friends hugged, after which Karen carefully primped to stop her ample bosom from escaping her dress. Sitting back down in a thronelike wicker chair, she quickly fanned herself with the beer menu and ran a finger around her neck to loosen the slightly sweaty, persimmon-orange bandanna knotted at her throat.

"Well, Teri June Inc. is back in business, I tell you!" exulted Karen, swinging the pounded-silver hoops dangling from her ears. "Hest, the whole Sara Duffy episode has been a gold mine for me. All that time I was afraid to come clean about my writing, and it turns out that my secret life has just been raw meat for the publicity agents. My confessional on 'Oprah' really put Teri June back on the best-seller list, I tell you! I have been book touring until my eyes bleed."

Hester smiled for her friend's good fortune, and eyed the golden beer in a half-full glass on the table in front of Karen. "Well, it's a warm day, what's good here?"

"I got the Portland Pilsener, and I think it's just about as good as those German lagers they charge $4 for on the deck at the Harborside," Karen said.

"Well, that's probably because it's most like the light and watery Blitz of your college days, dear heart," Hester said with a grin as she scanned the list.

Hester often surprised dining companions with her taste for dark beer, nurtured by growing up as the daughter of a confirmed Guinness man.

"I'm going to try the Sellwood Stout – it says it has 'rich aromas of burnt caramel and sarsaparilla,' " Hester enthused, adding as an afterthought, "I wonder if they could serve it over ice cream?"

When a hunky young barkeep with an Australian accent who called her "Luv" had taken Hester's order, the two friends compared their weeks.

"I have to say, Karen, I really didn't need to be involved in another murder case!" Hester moaned. "I don't *want* to be the 'Miss Marple librarian,' I just want my cozy old Portland back, with the dopey mayor on his clunky red Huffy, and the corny Rose Festival, and people getting all excited about Packy the elephant's birthday party at the zoo."

"Oh, Hester, I heard about Pieter van Dyke, and I'm so sorry," Karen responded, reaching out to hold her friend's hand. "I know how nice it is to come home to plain old Portland. I tell you, after doing book signings in New York, Atlanta and Philly all in one weekend, I can't tell you how much I appreciate the old hometown."

Karen sipped her beer and took off on another tangent.

"Do you know how much it costs to take a cab from the airport to midtown Manhattan? It was like 75 bucks – and I'm sure the Punjabi driver or whatever he was circled around the same block five times on the way to my hotel, unless there really *is* a Starbucks on every corner there now!"

Hester found herself tuning out her friend's monologue. She briefly considered taking Karen into her confidence about the weird discovery she'd made with the first-day cover. But Hester realized with some regret that her friend's long deception about her writing career had expended some of the basic currency of any friendship: trust. She bit back her urge to say something.

"And I swear, if the publisher wasn't picking up the tab, I couldn't afford chicken-fried steak in some of those East Coast cities," Karen went on.

As this statement sank in, Hester suddenly realized she was famished. Glancing at her wristwatch, she interrupted Karen.

"Say, Happy Hour ends in 20 minutes, do you want to get some Buffalo wings or something?"

Karen didn't miss a beat, waving to the barkeep, who seemed like her new best friend.

"Oh, Simon, could we get another round, and two orders of those Fusion Wings?" Turning back to Hester, she enthused, "Girl, Buffalo wings are as outdated as the bison of the Great Plains. These guys do 'em up with a combination of Thai peanut sauce, Korean kimchi and Fijian chili lime."

When their order had come and the barkeep started to rush back to the bar with a tray bearing their empty glasses, Hester had a sudden thought. She grabbed at his elbow as he started to skip away.

Unfortunately she caused him to stumble as he whirled back her direction. Grasping from her chair to steady him so he wouldn't drop the tray, she pulled him this way and that as the heavy pint glasses slid on his tray, until he came to a stop with his sinewy calves, bristling with curly, sun-bleached hair, straddling Hester's bare thighs just beneath the indigo-blue batik skirt she'd changed into before leaving the library.

Looking straight ahead at the waist of his day-glo orange and chartreuse board shorts four inches from her eyes she could read the label, "Quiksilver/Australia."

"Whoa, luv, we've only just met!" he chortled, peering down at her through the wraparound sunglasses he wore even indoors. "But I get off at 7, darlin'."

Hester, who knew her face was as red as the cayenne peppering the chicken wings sending up blissful aromas from her plate, quickly pushed her chair back three scoots.

"Ahem, I'm so sorry – I didn't mean to grab – Are you OK?" She dabbed at her temple with a napkin.

"Never better, luv, what can I do you for?" he leered.

Taking a quick gulp at her new beer – Willamette wheat ale this time – Hester pointed at a large television over the bar. "I just wanted to ask, before – before I – "

She shook her fiery locks. "Might it be possible to watch something other than wrestling?" she asked meekly. "I was thinking, maybe local news?"

Turning to Karen as the barkeep fiddled with a remote control from behind the counter, Hester shook her head. "I don't know about this new idea of having big TVs at bars. I can't believe it will catch on. Wouldn't it be more peaceful to just have some Pachelbel playing on the stereo?"

Karen rolled her eyes and was about to speak, but a newscast on the TV suddenly caught Hester's attention.

"…and from Forest Park, veteran reporter Misty Day has this latest update on the shocking Pieter van Dyke murder."

The spa-tanned face of KSNZ's former co-anchor filled the screen. With the unfortunate oversaturated color setting on the Blue Heron's cheap set, she resembled a tangerine wearing mascara.

"Thank you, Thaddeus. The roller-coaster ride continues in this breaking news story as word came today from Phil Bishop, founder of Oregon's Zeus sport-shoe empire, that although The Oregonian has called off its part of the contest, he is continuing to offer the $50,000 he had promised to the finder of the Rose Festival medallion. But instead of it being a prize, it will be a reward for return of what is now considered a potentially vital clue in the murder of one of Portland's leading citizens, philanthropist and civic leader Pieter van Dyke," the reporter said, biting off her words as the camera panned out to show her standing beneath the arch of the Thurman Street Bridge. Around her, people roved every which direction.

"And as you can see all around me, that news has brought out hundreds of civic-minded citizen sleuths who are combing this park in the belief that the medallion might not have wandered far from the ill-fated horseshoe pit that remains cordoned off behind me. Here's one hopeful searcher, Mr. Vernon Kayzer, a retired sanitation worker who drove 3 1/2 hours from Pendleton to search with his metal detector. Mr. Kayzer, what are your hopes?"

A man with a military crew cut, a nasal voice and a turquoise track suit loomed into the picture.

"Well, Misty, with my trusty machine here I've found everything from Indian Head nickels on the beach at Yachats to a jarful of pennies buried in a schoolyard in Hermiston, so I figure I might just be the one to help crack this murder case – and if I get the $50,000 reward, I personally pledge 1 percent of it to the Future Numismatists of America."

The camera cut back to a bored-looking Misty Day, caught rolling her eyes before she snapped back to her on-air persona.

"That's a noble idea, Mr. Kayzer. Now, Thaddeus, I have my own discovery to reveal about this corner of Forest Park. It's not the first time it has figured in an infamous Portland murder."

She paused to arch a heavily penciled eyebrow before continuing.

"Today I came across a small historical marker, hidden among the bushes here, documenting how this was the 1850 land claim of one Danford Balch. He settled here with his wife and nine children, not far from the claim of a family named Stump, with whom the Balches did not get along. In true Shakespearean fashion, the Stumps' eldest son, Mortimer, eloped with Balch's 16-year-old daughter, after which Balch shot and killed him. As a result, Danford Balch was the first person to be legally hanged in Portland. True story."

The camera zoomed in on Day's stern face.

"So, Thaddeus," she concluded, almost managing to furrow her overtucked brow, "this isn't the first time this quiet nook of Forest Park has figured in a macabre story of murder. And if the Zeus Corporation's reward leads to conviction of another killer, it might once again lead to a public hanging for a murder linked to the old Balch Place. For KSNZ, I'm Misty Day."

Dumbfounded, Hester stared at the TV. Then, as if in a trance, she stood, pointed to the continuing newscast and spoke loudly to the two other tables of Happy Hour revelers.

"I want to say for the record that, first, anybody who went to middle school in Portland was taught all about Danford Balch and his son-in-law – though maybe Misty skipped class that day – and, two, Oregon hasn't had hanging as a method of execution since 1931!"

Karen White sat with her hand splayed across her downcast eyes. The other bar patrons stared silently at Hester.

Finally looking up, Karen rose, scooped the chicken wings on to one platter, grabbed their beers and toe-walked Hester quickly across the pub and through an open French door to an outdoor balcony.

Pushing Hester into a seat beneath a burnt-orange canvas umbrella at a table with a downhill view toward the river, Karen handed Hester her beer.

"Some people might say you've had too much, but I think you haven't had enough," Karen told her old friend. "Chugalug, dear heart."

Hester took a gulp of beer as Karen gestured with a wing bone at the weary librarian.

70

"In fact, I think all this murder business has you taking life so seriously you haven't had much fun on several fronts for too long," Karen said, finally tugging at the knot and tossing her bandanna on the table in a gesture of liberation. "For one thing, your little fling – or I might say, '*flingus interrupttus*' – with Clarence Darrow has you all uptight."

"Clarence was his great, great uncle or something, and you know his name is Nate," Hester rejoined with a minor pout.

"Fine, but you can't tell me that little Marx Brothers physical comedy act in there with our Australian buddy didn't have some Freudian element," Karen retorted. "You, girlfriend, need someone in your bed other than that shedding cat of yours."

Hester stared silently at Portland's West Hills, where the glare of the lowering sun through shimmering waves of heat rising off downtown created the optical illusion of flames racing along the ridgeline.

As she brooded on Karen's goading, something else niggled at Hester's consciousness. A tinny sound came and went from down toward the river, and then got louder, finally transforming into music with a heavy Latin beat.

Karen, too, was peering toward the Willamette when finally the source of the music appeared through a break in the bigleaf maples. At first, it was like a mirage: an old riverboat, like something from a Mark Twain story.

Then it came to them both in a flash.

"It's the Rose! The old stern-wheeler that gives river tours," Karen exclaimed. "Oh, I've heard about this, they're doing Sunset Macarena Cruises."

The Latin song and dance craze, the Macarena, had been sweeping the world in recent months. Suddenly, Karen's eyes narrowed.

"That's it! It's exactly what you need! I'm brilliant!"

Hester shot a veiled look at her friend. "Oh, Karen, I couldn't – "

"Of course you could!" Karen shot back. "And in this summery weather, that boat is going to be crawling with hot men! Hester, sweetie, I'm booking us a cruise!"

Chapter Fourteen

An hour later, Hester had lucked into an easy parking space on maple-lined Everett Street and was trying to remember if she had any food in her fridge as she trudged up the front steps of the Luxor, her Egyptian-themed apartment house in the Northwest neighborhood.

"Good evening, Ramses," she called out, a habit she had picked up from watching too many old movies in which New York socialites greeted their uniformed doormen as they came and went. But in Hester's case, her greeting was to the cement Egyptian pharaoh figure over the doorway.

As she ducked through the front door and past the potted palm in the elephant-foot planter, the elevator's door was just swinging closed.

"Hold the elevator!" Hester called, knowing she was taking a chance that there was only one occupant. The Luxor's tiny, elderly elevator, with its manually operated accordion-cage safety gate and outer door that swung out instead of sliding together in the middle, could hold only two passengers. "And even those had better be of compatible body-mass ratio," she often warned friends.

The inner door ratcheted open – there must be room! – and the outer door swung out toward her. Hester ducked in.

The signature aroma of bay rum and hot pepperoni told her who it was before she'd even looked up to meet the eyes of Nate Darrow.

"Gosh! We meet again," Hester grinned self-consciously, twisting her body sideways so Darrow could hold his big pizza box close to horizontal while she punched the button for "three."

Pizza was his all-too-usual dinner from Escape From New York, the counterculture pizza joint up on 23rd named for a bad Kurt Russell movie from the '80s. The pizza joint's neon Statue of Liberty sign was a neighborhood icon.

"Hester! How was your afternoon?" Darrow inquired.

She opened her mouth but realized she had to stop to think about her answer. Finally, she spoke.

"Well, actually, it was kind of weird, if you want to know the truth." She paused and looked into his hazel eyes. As usual, she felt a little extra flip-flop as their eyes locked. Was this what the French called a frisson? Hester shook herself out of overanalyzing.

"As a matter of fact, something came up that I probably need to talk to you about," she said in a rush, as the old lift clinked and clanked slowly upward. "Something – " she hesitated, then plunged ahead. "Something to do with that Charbonneau character."

A jolt like a painful memory crossed Darrow's face. When it became apparent Hester wasn't ready to say more, he crinkled his forehead. "So, have you eaten?" Bobbing the box up and down in his hands and nodding at it, he added, "Why don't you come on up?"

Hester hesitated.

"Oh, you know I like to watch my girlish figure." A facetious tone, then a note of seriousness as she added, "And Bingle T. is probably ready to eat his foot."

She referred to the 28-pound Maine Coon cat with whom she shared an apartment, whose constant crooning as a kitten got him named after Bing Crosby. The initial "T," for "Troublemaker," came later, because of his tendency to escape from her apartment and show up in the most unlikely of places.

Hester cogitated, feeling her stomach rumble. In a sudden moment of rebellion against dieting – and letting a fuzzy feline rule her life – she turned back to Darrow. "Actually, pizza sounds great! The Wiener Dog seems like a long time ago, and all I've had since then was a couple of kimchi chicken wings that were, frankly, kind of nasty."

Darrow's eyes brightened. "If you want to stop in and feed the cat, I'll keep the pizza warm," he offered.

But Hester was resolute, punching the "4" button when the elevator stopped at her floor.

"No, he'll survive. I've had him on a diet anyway ever since Mr. Podlodowski the janitor was prompted to do his Porky Pig imitation the last time he came to fix my kitchen fan. He saw Bingle T. and made some rude comment about how 'if that big fella had been born over at Good Samaritan they'd have had to charge for triplets,'" referring to the hospital a few blocks away.

Darrow bit back a grin as Hester mused.

"You know, I've really cut back his crunchies – he's a terrible 24-hour snacker – and I think he's still gaining weight!"

Now a look of mild alarm crossed Nate's face, but as Hester caught his eyes again, the detective put on his best look of poker-face innocence.

"Imagine that!" he commiserated as the elevator finally clunked to a stop at his floor.

Darrow's apartment was transformed since Hester had peeked in shortly after he had arrived four months earlier. As he passed the dining nook, he slid the big pizza box onto a dark walnut British pub table, which Hester immediately admired for its clever old-school design, with extra leaves that slid out to seat more dinner guests.

"Got that in Sellwood," Darrow told her as he gestured her to a chair at the table, then peeled off his sport coat and hung it on a brass rack in a corner.

The bricks-and-boards bookcase along one wall held a sizable collection of vinyl LP records, their jackets leaning up against a high-quality receiver and turntable like what her dad used to play his Sousa marches on before her mother had finally nudged him over to compact discs and a good set of headphones.

"And that was my father's stereo outfit, too high quality to give up in favor of soulless digital," he said, noting Hester's fascination. Darrow had inherited it when his parents had died in a car crash when he was in college.

Cocking his head with a sudden thought, he grabbed an LP off the shelf, shook the record from its sleeve, deftly dropped it onto the turntable, flicked the power button and eased the needle into the grooves. The mellow piano playing of Vince Guaraldi started to tinkle softly from a big Advent speaker next to the shelves.

Hester tilted her head back in appreciation, gazing across to a wall with a large framed print of van Gogh's "Wheatfield with Cypresses." Fanciful, Dr. Seuss-like trees and golden stalks of grain swayed beneath a blissfully blue French sky.

Darrow had disappeared into the kitchen but now reappeared with a slightly dripping longneck beer bottle in each hand.

"The one culinary rule in Chez Darrow is that beer is the perfect pairing with pizza," he announced as if emceeing a cable-TV food show. "And I happen to have put a new batch of my home brew in to chill when I left this morning. Will you try one with me?"

At Hester's nod, he popped the tops using a wall-mounted bottle capper at the kitchen's entrance that was etched with the message, "Souvenir of Wall Drug, South Dakota."

Hester studied the beer bottle Darrow handed her. "Rosabella Amber Ale," the obviously homemade label said. Beneath a drawing of an old-fashioned looking sailboat was the legend "A full-keeled brew from Darrow Brewing, Portland, Oregon."

Shifting her eye from the bottle to Darrow, who was just finishing a first swig with a contemplative swirl through his cheeks, Hester raised the beer in one hand and pointed curiously at the label.

"Rosabella is my uncle's boat, named from a wonderful old sea chantey – the boat I've sailed on around Vancouver Island and down in the Sea of Cortez," Nate explained. "The artwork is by my 10-year-old niece, so be kind."

"No, I think it's quite good. I'm just mildly bemused at witnessing another Nathaniel Darrow fanaticism," Hester said with a smile in her eye as she took an appreciative sip.

Darrow handed her a plate and napkin, then held the box while Hester scooped up a pizza slice, making sure she didn't lose too many of the black olives.

As the spicy aroma filled her head and Hester took her first bite, a clatter from Darrow's hallway caught their attention.

"What the…?" Darrow said as he set down the pizza box and strode into the short hall to investigate.

Hester heard a door open, then a confused "Whoa!" from Nate combined with a familiar, excited feline trilling, and suddenly her fluffy, gray-and-black striped cat with the large green eyes was scooting around the corner and leaping into her lap.

"Bingle T., how on earth?" Hester cried, as the big cat unceremoniously sniffed at her pizza slice, snagged a piece of pepperoni in his teeth and gobbled it down with hardly stopping to chew. "How did you get here?"

"Well, to paraphrase an old Beatles song, 'He came in through the bathroom window!'" Darrow said in answer to her question.

"And don't worry, all we heard was my can of Barbasol getting knocked off the windowsill."

"But, but..." was all a dumbfounded Hester could manage as her ravenous cat helped himself to another piece of pepperoni from her forgotten pizza.

"Apparently he has figured out how to get out your bathroom window and climb up to mine using the ivy and pipes on the wall in the air shaft," Darrow informed her.

A dawning look of comprehension on Hester's face slowly turned to suspicion.

"Wait, how have you figured this out so quickly?" Her eyes flitted between her neighbor and her cat, who was suddenly looking all too at-home in these surroundings.

Darrow's lips came together as if he were about to whistle. He looked down and reached over to scratch the big cat behind the ears. A throaty purr immediately rose from Bingle T.

"Cheese it, the cops, Bing boy!" Darrow hissed in his best Edward G. Robinson imitation.

"You're telling me this isn't the first time he's DONE THIS?"

Hester's incredulity warmed the room a noticeable five degrees, Darrow thought.

"Well, apparently he likes pepperoni, as you might notice," Darrow explained.

"But, but – when?"

"Remember that time last week I knocked on your door and said I found him in the hallway? And another time old Podlodowski unlocked your place and let me pop him back inside."

Hester was now turning as red as the third piece of pepperoni her cat was about to snitch.

"And why on earth didn't you TELL ME THE TRUTH?" she spluttered.

With lower lip protruding, Darrow looked like a guilty second-grader caught taking an extra gumdrop from the teacher's secret stash. After wagging his head back and forth a few times, he explained.

"Because I thought you'd get all upset about it! And I guess I called *that one* right," he said, muttering this last part to the cat.

Returning to address his human neighbor, he added, "And it was kind of nice having the company!"

Hester stared up at an old water stain in the ceiling as she blew her breath out through clenched teeth, then let her peeve evaporate with a sigh as she deftly moved the pizza out of Bingle T.'s reach before he could get a fourth pepperoni.

"You terrible, horrible cat!" she said, trying unsuccessfully to stifle the mirth sneaking into her voice. Then, to Darrow, "Do you know he once got into the trunk of a neighbor's car when they were packing for the beach and I had to drive 20 miles down Highway 26 to retrieve him when they stopped for gas?"

Darrow, relieved that he seemed forgiven, returned to gobbling pizza.

Pausing to look at her neighbor again, Hester's eyes wandered down to his service revolver in a shoulder holster.

"You ever shoot that thing?" she asked, ready to change the subject.

Darrow blanched and slapped his forehead, realizing he'd forgotten his usual routine of locking the gun in his nightstand drawer the moment he stepped in the door.

"Well, actually I don't even keep it loaded most days," he called back, having moved quickly into the next room to peel off the shoulder harness. Beyond the wall and through the open door, she heard him add,

"I'm not very good at following procedures, I'm afraid." A silent pause. "I'm a terrible policeman, really."

Hester smiled at that admission. He might not follow all procedures, but she wasn't sure that made him a bad policeman. The more she got to know him, she was pretty sure Darrow felt the same way.

"I probably do enough procedure following for the both of us," she said to herself, reflecting on her day as she opened the pizza box and helped herself to a fresh slice.

"What's that you say?" Nate asked as he returned and plunked down in a dining chair of carved wood and forest-green leather.

"Actually, I was just thinking I need to depart from procedures myself and tell you about something I haven't even told my bosses yet," Hester said, taking a quick gulp of her neighbor's refreshingly hoppy home brew to bolster her resolve.

It was Darrow's turn to look quizzical as he plucked a piece of slightly burnt pepperoni from the top of the pizza and surreptitiously handed it to the cat that was now furiously polishing his ankles.

By the time Hester had filled Darrow in on the afternoon's latest discovery with the McLoughlin Collection, cold grease stains had spread across the bottom of the cardboard pizza box like nimbus clouds across a March sky.

Darrow gave a long, low whistle.

"Pomp Charbonneau is a name I really didn't need to have come up in my dinnertime conversation, I have to tell you, Miss Marple," Darrow said.

"I'll kick you in the shins if you call me that again," Hester said coquettishly, but with a steely cast in her eye that Darrow couldn't miss.

"Guess how I spent my whole afternoon," he continued. "Running all over Greater Portland trying to find our friend Pomp Charbonneau."

He shook his head at the recollection.

"We did figure out that he's a swing-shift printer at The Oregonian, but when I dropped by there the deputy publisher who saw 'All The President's Men' a few too many times got all First Amendment on me and demanded a warrant before they'd even give me the guy's phone number. So I cruised out to Newberg to visit the address we dug up from state tax records only to find it was one of those private mailbox centers in a strip mall between a KFC and a nail salon. I got pepperoni tonight because I needed something to help get the 'bucket o' chicken' smell out of my sinuses after sitting outside the stupid mailbox place for two hours hoping the guy would stop in to pick up his Publisher's Clearing House mailer. He could already be a millionaire, you know, and he doesn't even seem to care."

Darrow sighed and took a long swallow of his beer. "Mmm, that came out pretty nicely," he murmured appreciatively to the ceiling before continuing.

"So now, Hester, from what you tell me, it sounds like Charbonneau not only might know something about the gun that killed Pieter van Dyke, but might somehow also be mixed up in, what, the *counterfeiting* of a valuable library artifact? Some sort of stamp-collector's envelope thingy that once belonged to van Dyke's father?"

Darrow looked into her blue eyes with that gaze that Hester found hard to take calmly.

"These are some really weird tea leaves we've got to read here, wouldn't you say?" he said with finality.

Hester, who had been taking it all in with her chin in her hand, finally spoke up.

"OK, I can see that because Charbonneau is a printer he could have faked the first day cover – but why add a third person? And how in the name of heaven did he make the switch? I vaguely recall Pim telling me he is a master printer and uses an art-quality technique of some kind… But, I've met him. He's not master-criminal material. It was the third guy in the boat that tipped us off it was a fake."

"Lord knows, an accomplice inside?" Darrow said. "But first tell me how much that first-day cover was worth – the original. Was it worth stealing?"

Hester blanched and bit her lip.

Darrow knitted his brow and peered at her. "Hester?"

"Oh, dear, this isn't going to play well for the library, I'm afraid," she said. "But I suppose it's going to come out one way or another now."

Darrow waited silently, drawing rings in the condensation on his beer bottle as he waited for her to go on.

Drawing a deep breath, Hester forged on.

"You know this isn't my department but it doesn't take long to figure out that considering the value of some of the artifacts in the McLoughlin Collection, the library has woefully underinvested in security."

"That doesn't sound good," Darrow said, pinching the bridge of his nose between thumb and forefinger. "Come on, let's have the bad news."

"Well, it's nothing definitive, but my Dad knows a stamp dealer out by Lloyd Center, so I gave him a call this afternoon and he happened to have heard about a recent auction of one of the few other 'Flying Canoe' covers," Hester said.

Gulping, she added, "It sold for six figures. He was pretty sure it was over $250,000."

Chapter Fifteen

By the time he left his job in the color-camera back shop at *The Oregonian* that night, Pomp Charbonneau had solved several mini-crises that had threatened to stop the Friday morning newspaper from going to press.

The sports editor had been tearing out what little was left of his hair because a centerpiece photo of an Oregon Ducks athlete had made the team colors appear to be brown and orange instead of green and yellow.

But the full-page Meier & Frank department store ad in which the men's briefs looked Pepto-Bismol pink was the biggest challenge. Nobody was going to pay for that, and it meant thousands to the newspaper.

As usual, the bosses had turned to their best print-shop wizard to save the day.

On his 45-minute drive home, Charbonneau made a quick stop at his private mailbox and was pleased to find another order from a Portland artist for 25 giclée prints of the oil paintings she made featuring montages of balsamroot blossoms, a prolific wildflower that carpeted hillsides on the sunny side of the Columbia Gorge.

The headlights of his old truck reflected on the silvery sides of his trailer and in the eyes of a big raccoon as he pulled to a stop at the edge of a Willamette Valley vineyard. Looking up, he saw the seven stars of the Pleiades pulsing in and out of focus in the darkening sky.

Charbonneau stepped inside briefly, rummaged through his tiny fridge, pulled out a homemade venison meat pie, popped it into the propane oven, and then set a plate of yesterday's leftovers on the front step for the raccoon before crossing his clearing to a small barn.

After a steamy shower in the bathroom he'd plumbed himself, he rubbed a towel over his dark, wet hair and pulled it back into a ponytail as he stepped into the cool sanctuary of his winery, which occupied half the barn.

Sniffing happily at the heady sour-tart aroma of fermenting grapes, Charbonneau picked an old canoe paddle off a hook on the wall, lifted a net of cheesecloth from atop a stainless steel vat and vigorously stirred, breaking up the cap of grape skins and pulp that had floated to the top of his newest red.

While others used special metal paddles purchased from wine-supply warehouses for this daily chore, Pomp preferred the old wooden paddle he had used on many a canoe trip exploring sloughs along the lower Columbia. That it might not be perfectly sterile, perhaps explaining why several of his wines had gone "off," mattered less to him than the character it added.

Replacing the cheesecloth over the vat, he stopped at a small table, polished a wineglass with a cotton towel, then pulled a bung from a purple-stained oak barrel and used a pipette "thief" to pull a sample of merlot and transfer it to the glass.

He held the glass up to the single light bulb hanging from above, swirled the ruby liquid and then took a deep, satisfying sniff before stepping back into the other half of the barn and pulling the door securely closed behind him.

The rest of the barn was divided into two quarters: his print shop and his collection room.

This was the latter. He plopped down in an old leather recliner to sip his wine and admire the wall hung with oiled iron animal traps, more canoe paddles of all sizes, tomahawks from the Shoshone Tribe, ancient snowshoes, and his collection of vintage firearms – all authentic. The library had its McLoughlin Collection. This was the Charbonneau Collection.

Nearest his chair was a rough wooden wall of framed photos of his four ex-wives and eight children. His first wife bore him no offspring, or there'd have been more.

"Ah, you slacker, you," he said to her photo as he swirled the wine under his nose.

Charbonneau's one big regret was that he didn't see more of his kids. He scanned their framed school photos. At top were the oldest, Pomp Jr., Sacajawea and Clark, a trio of dashing, dark-eyed teens. Next were Wife No. 3's preteen offspring, T.J. (for Thomas Jefferson), and the girl, Montana. At the bottom were Wife No. 4's little girl, Dakota, and the preschool twins, Jean and Baptiste.

Also there: framed mementos, such as a sample of the $2 bills he had printed up and regularly handed out to the homeless back in D.C. before some Starbucks cashier had noticed she had a till full of bills on which Thomas Jefferson sported a Snidely Whiplash mustache.

About that time, Wife No. 4 had thrown him out, so Charbonneau had decided it might be a good idea to move to the West Coast before the Secret Service tracked him down. When he scanned a map, the nearby community of Charbonneau, Oregon, had originally drawn him to the Portland area.

He sipped the merlot – good plummy notes developing, he noticed – and remembered the printing order he'd stuffed in a pocket.

He pulled it out and mentally calculated the income it would bring. Thank God, maybe he'd keep the collection agencies at bay for another month. Child-support was killing him.

Not only that, but Pomp Jr. was graduating from high school on Sunday back in Virginia and Dad had promised him a Trans Am for graduation. While Charbonneau tended to live for today and didn't worry much about his children's future, a Charbonneau promise meant something.

Pushing himself out of the armchair, he stepped through another door, into his print shop.

A look at his watch told him he had a few minutes before his dinner would be hot. Thinking ahead to the weekend when he'd tackle the art prints, he set his wineglass safely out of the way and busied himself cleaning up from his last job: the Flying Canoe first-day cover.

A grin flashed across his face as he studied the extra copy he'd kept to frame for his wall. He and his ancestors had long resented the short shrift historians gave Toussaint. From the time he was knee-high to his grandfather, Pomp had heard the family's belief that the Corps of Discovery should have been known as the Lewis, Clark *and Charbonneau* Expedition.

So Pomp had exercised his wicked sense of humor and put Toussaint in the canoe, too, when he replicated the Flying Canoe first-day cover for Pieter van Dyke.

Chapter Sixteen

Friday, June 14

At 8 a.m., traffic into the city was all clogged up on the downhill bends of the Sunset Highway just before the tunnel, but it didn't bother Nate Darrow. He took pleasure as he shifted into fourth gear and listened to the throaty roar of his classic silver Volvo 1800 coupe as it rocketed up the hill in the opposite direction, toward Portland's western suburbs.

Darrow's old car was one of his few material possessions in which he invested real pride, one of the Seven Deadly Sins his Lutheran grandmother had warned him about.

He'd worked the summer after high school on a crab boat out of the Oregon Coast town of Newport to buy the used car, a symbol of panache that had set him apart from school chums who drove hulking Impalas and old Beetles.

He called his car "Sven," in honor of its Swedish heritage, which it shared with Darrow's mother's family, the Boresons. He was reminded of that heritage every time he looked at the parts bill when his car needed a repair – more and more often, now that it was 30 years old.

"They have to charge so much because some guy named Ole rows the parts across from Stockholm," he grumbled jokingly to friends.

A recent rebore meant this was one of those periods when his bank balance was low but he could step on Sven's accelerator and not have to worry about sounds from under the hood like someone choking on lutefisk.

And he always took pleasure in the car's red leather bucket seats, wood-trimmed dashboard, and sleek profile.

"It's like Bond's original Aston-Martin, just without the machine guns or the smoke-screen thing," he had boasted to Harry Harrington.

"That kind of depends on how much oil Sven is burning on any particular day, Nate," Harry had replied.

This sun-drenched morning was supposed to be his half-day off, but Darrow was pursuing a hunch on how to track down the elusive Pomp Charbonneau without having to wait for a stakeout outside The Oregonian that night. With Hester's revelations about his apparent involvement in forgery, Charbonneau was definitely now a "person of interest."

Recalling that the printer also dabbled at winemaking, Darrow had phoned his brother, Bud, after saying goodnight to Hester the previous night.

"If Charbonneau is part of the winemaking scene out in the West Valley, my brother will know him," he'd assured Hester.

Bud Darrow had chosen to carry on the "family business," as he put it. The two boys had heard their father, an Oregon State viticulture professor, wax eloquently and endlessly about the Willamette Valley's suitability for growing cooler-climate wine grapes such as pinot noir and pinot gris. While his father's involvement in Oregon's nascent wine industry in the 1970s had been limited to academics and bringing home bottles to sample around the family dinner table, from the early 1980s Bud had been one of the region's rising winemaking stars. He had his winery in the little village of Carlton, north of McMinnville, where the town's tall grain elevator now cast its shadow on a growing number of tony tasting rooms along the two blocks of "downtown."

"Yeah, I've met Charbonneau," Bud Darrow responded on the phone to Nate's inquiry. Bud's voice was old cigar to Nate's coffee and cream.

"He's kind of a survivalist nut. Has it in his head he can do a great Bordeaux blend here, but he just can't get his Cab to ripen in the little gulch he's farming. Frost comes too soon."

"Can you tell me where he lives?" Nate pressed.

"Oh, golly, he's out below Ribbon Ridge. Makes wine in a barn he bought from old Billy Brickhouse, and lives in an Airstream trailer next to

Billy's chardonnay vineyard. But the roads out there are like a rabbit warren, you'll never find it on your own."

"What if I talked to this Billy fellow? Could he show me? It's kind of urgent."

"Naw, don't bother old Billy. He's got phylloxera in his best pinot patch and the man's a basket case right now. Tell you what, come out for breakfast tomorrow and afterward I'll run you out there. I've got to pick up a load of cow dung up in Yamhill anyway. Solstice is coming, you know."

As Nate turned Sven past the Beaverton malls to weave his way toward the rural valley, he pondered the phenomenon that was his big brother. Two years earlier, Bud Darrow, who had earned a double major in philosophy and viticulture at U.C. Davis, had converted his winery to biodynamics, an agricultural protocol posited in the 1920s by Austrian philosopher Rudolf Steiner. It combined organic sciences with mysticism, which in practical purposes meant that, among other things, Bud planted his vines by the light of the full moon and buried manure in old cow horns to ferment for six months before being dug up every solstice and used as fertilizer.

Skeptical colleagues tongue-in-cheekily referred to his brother's Wahoo Vineyards as "Woo Woo Winery." Nate tried to reserve judgment.

"If nothing else, all the rules about pruning on the Feast of St. Stephen and spraying fertilizer on Epiphany mean your brother's out in his vineyard paying a whole lot more attention to the plants than those absentee owners who fly in twice a year from California," Nate had heard from the proprietor at his favorite Portland wine shop. "And healthy vines make good wine."

Sometimes, though, Bud seemed to be leading the parade of Oregon's growing cadre of crystal healers and Maypole dancers, Nate thought. He'd gobbled a piece of cold pizza before leaving home, since Bud had promised a "tofu-kale free-range scramble" for breakfast.

A half-hour later, Nate was surreptitiously picking the green and gray bits out of his eggs as Bud and his wife, Betty, regaled him with the latest lacrosse-field achievements of Nate's 13-year-old nephew, Dylan.

Their 10-year-old daughter, still in her nightie, sat uncommunicatively nearby with a morose look on her face as she munched through a bowl of granola.

"Sophy's not really a morning person," her mother explained.

As Nate tried to smile appreciatively, a green-and-white sheriff's cruiser pulled slowly into the old yellow farmhouse's gravel drive just behind the silver Volvo.

"Well, hey, it's Wayne Jordan," said Bud, a two-inches shorter, 20-pounds heavier, crew-cut version of his brother. This morning Bud was outfitted in Lee jeans and an L.L. Bean flannel shirt in contrast to Nate's collegiate wardrobe of checked Oxford shirt, corduroy trousers and argyle socks.

Nate stood to shake hands as the uniformed deputy from the Washington County Sheriff's Office climbed the creaky steps to the screened sun porch where they were breakfasting.

"I was just passing and saw the old Finnish flivver," smiled the blond, freckled deputy, a former colleague of Nate's from his early days on the force in Ashland, near Oregon's southern border. Jordan could never seem to keep straight which Scandinavian country built Volvos.

"Wayne, what a nice surprise," Nate responded as Betty, a farm wife whose milky complexion and calm demeanor seemed to draw nourishment from the nature around her, sprang to the kitchen for an extra coffee cup.

As the two old friends caught up over shade-grown, fair-trade Costa Rican dark roast – Bud had long ago spoiled his brother for the instant coffee he'd consumed in college – Nate got around to telling a little about his interest in Pomp Charbonneau.

"I know where that wacko lives," Jordan responded. "I had to assist once with a health-department enforcement when he staged an unlicensed possum roast during our big Memorial Day wine tour. He claimed it was the perfect pairing with his new red blend. But people were throwing up."

As Jordan finished off a second helping of scrambled eggs, with kale bits stuck in his teeth to show for it, he added, "Hey, Nate, I'm heading out past Ribbon Ridge to do a welfare check on someone's grandmother – I could lead you to Charbonneau's place."

Bud Darrow happily consented to pass off that duty, quipping, "A truckload of steaming cow shit waits for no man."

Ten minutes later Nate was downshifting the Volvo for the umpteenth turn along the narrow country roads, weaving among hazelnut orchards, patches of Douglas-fir forest and sunny hillsides of wine grapes.

A cloud of dust raised by the sheriff's cruiser signaled that the road turned to gravel ahead. In another 500 feet, Nate followed as the cruiser turned into a grassy drive and slowly rocked and rolled for five minutes along the edge of a vineyard thick with emerald green, heart-shaped leaves and corkscrewing tendrils climbing wires toward the sky.

At a clearing, red taillights flashed through dust as Jordan pulled up alongside a gleaming silver travel trailer, its front end supported by cinder blocks, with small red-white-and-blue flags – one American, one French – fluttering from staffs above the door.

"My brother was right, I'd never have found this place," Nate said as the two men climbed out of their cars. "Wayne, thanks for the help, but you really don't need to stop. I just need to talk to this guy."

"Not a problem, it's my neighborhood. Let's see if ol' Pomp is home," replied the deputy, reverting to his "line of duty" protocol, fingering the baton on his belt and unsnapping his sidearm holster as he stepped to the door of the trailer and gave a polite rap.

The only sound was the trilling "chirree" of a red-winged blackbird from a cattail marsh across the road.

Jordan rapped harder. "Sheriff's deputy, Mr. Charbonneau!" he called, his voice echoing away into the vineyard.

Across the clearing, an unseen rusty door hinge slowly creaked from a small barn that was once cherry red but was now faded to match the wild pink roses edging a nearby ditch.

The two men exchanged glances, then nodded and walked toward the barn. Darrow reached under his sport coat and put his hand on his service revolver, trying to remember if he'd loaded it that morning.

They were halfway across the clearing when a diesel engine chugged to life from the far side of the building. In another instant, an ancient flatbed truck with rounded, rusting green fenders careened into sight, speeding away down a narrow, grassy lane between vineyard rows.

Darrow threw up his arms and vainly shouted, "Stop! Police!"

He ran to look down the gap between grapevines, hoping to be able to identify the truck. It looked like an old Chevy, probably built about the same time Darrow was born. Its knobby tires threw bits of sod high into the air as it sped away.

His eyes widened at what else he saw: Just turning into the lane from the opposite direction was a small tractor pulling a trailer full of vineyard clippings. On the side of the trailer's wooden box was stenciled in large letters, "Brickhouse Vineyards."

Old Billy Brickhouse barely had time to react to the oncoming flatbed. He spun the tractor's wheel and plowed sideways into the ditch. His trailer turned on its side.

The speeding truck caromed to the right and flattened the tall, crossed poles supporting the end of a vineyard row. It continued along the row, taking down two more sets of stout poles, each with a loud pop, before lurching to a stop with tangled ribbons of wire and shredded grapevines protruding from every wheel well.

Now Darrow could make out the hand-painted sign on the truck's door: "Charbonneau Cellars: For the amour of the grape."

Turning to Deputy Jordan, he said, "I think we're going to do more than just ask a few questions of Mr. Charbonneau."

Chapter Seventeen

"Woo hoo, did you see this?!" Pim asked excitedly, waving at a large photo on the front page of *The Oregonian* as she sat in the bookmobile's brown vinyl driver seat that morning at the edge of Alberta Park.

Sunshine, filtered by the Northeast Portland park's lovely grove of tall firs, streamed in the open window next to her, adding an extra glow to her canary-yellow Aloha shirt decorated with fire-breathing tiki gods.

The air was still refreshingly cool at 10 a.m., but the sun's intensity promised a warm June day to come, with a forecast in the mid-70s.

"Look, it's Schnitzel, the Wiener Dog restaurant's mascot, on the front page!" Peering owlishly at the photo caption, she added, "And oh my golly, Hester – he found the Rose Medallion!"

A phone call from the bookmobile barn early that morning had informed Hester that the police were done with their forensic work and that the magenta bus could return to service. In a quick call to Pim, they'd decided to go ahead and do the usual Friday rounds. To Hester, a bit of normal routine sounded good at the end of the discombobulating week.

"Goodness, how did a dachshund find the Rose Medallion?" Hester marveled, happy for the conversation while she tidied the shelves as they waited for the first patrons to arrive. Pim continued reading, mumbling quietly to herself in a manner Hester had come to find endearing over the years.

"Whoa, what a story! The Rajneeshees even got involved!"

"Oh, dear, don't tell me the police chief and the dreadful TV news people were right all along?"

"No, no, it says here the cymbal clinkers showed up in their peacemobile VW bus yesterday afternoon at Forest Park for their annual squirrel feed…"

"They eat *squirrels*?" Hester interjected, disgust twisting her features.

"No, no, no – they bring a big bag of dried corn they've raised on their organic farm and feed it *to* the squirrels in the park! How about that? Every once in a while those folks don't sound so bad."

"Oh. So what did that have to do with Schnitzel the wiener dog?"

"Well, that's where the story gets good," Pim said, twisting around in her seat like an excited child to face Hester. "While the peacemobile crowd is getting mobbed by squirrels under the Thurman Bridge, you have to remember that the park is still crawling with medallion hunters, thanks to that Zeus Shoes guy. In fact, I was out there for an hour yesterday myself with Lilly Pilly, because that little dog has dug up the most amazing things over the years, but we didn't have any luck," Pim said, using her pet name for her own canine housemate, Queen Liliuokalani.

"And?" Hester cocked an eyebrow.

"So I guess the cook from the Wiener Dog had the same idea, and he's there with Schnitzel, who's actually the latest in a long line of Schnitzel dogs, the first of which was the actual model for the Wiener Dog signs. *There's* something to know about the next time you play Portland Trivia!" Pim added, quelled from continuing the line of thought only by Hester's momentary glower of impatience.

"Anyway, I guess when Schnitzel saw all the squirrels, he went crackers and chased one into the brush. And when he comes back out, guess what's in his mouth? The Rose Medallion, hanging on a ribbon!"

A lilting "Hellooo?" interrupted Pim's triumphant conclusion to the story as a head popped in through the open rear door and the day's first bookmobile patron climbed aboard.

Maybelle Adams ran a soul-food café over on Martin Luther King Jr. Boulevard, and earned a top spot in the "Bookmobile Patron Hall of Fame" because she never showed up empty-handed.

"I have a couple slices of sweet potato pie for you ladies, just because I know you've had a difficult week and you need to keep your strength up!" she said, handing over a paper plate wrapped in foil as she squeezed into the bus, her full figure wrapped in a colorful African caftan. Her voice always rang like the Liberty bell through the small space.

"Ah, Maybelle, I have a new Ann Rule for you!" Hester responded to her most fervent True Crime reader. "It's about that grisly quadruple-murder cannibalism case in Cleveland. I couldn't stand to read more than a chapter, but I think it's right up your alley."

"Just call me Grisly Adams!" the grandmother of six chortled with a Cheshire-cat grin.

The morning went quickly, with two more stops, first at the Albina housing projects, then a quick stop at a St. Johns old-folks' home where Hester delivered a big bag of what she called "bodice buster" paperbacks to the lobby and picked up another bag of returns. Like many senior-living facilities, this one was 90 percent women, many of whom still enjoyed a titillating tale.

"Oh, and I was glad to see Mrs. O'Donnell so I could clue her in to that rooty-tooty new Nora Roberts – another of her Ireland romances – before the rotten desk clerk could snitch it," Hester reported happily as Pim guided the diesel-belching bus toward their lunch stop.

The Motormouth Drive-in on Interstate Avenue was another of Pim's Portland favorites, a vintage relic of the 1950s that still had carhop service and tinny-sounding speakers on which you could place your order. They also had a fish sandwich and tangy coleslaw that kept Hester happy while Pim gobbled her usual Megaburger.

"Oh drat, we can't do the carhop service today, we won't fit under the carport awning with these doggone canoes on the roof," Pim scowled.

Hester had momentarily forgotten that the bookmobile still carried the dugout canoes from the Rose Festival parade.

"We might as well leave them on there for the team-building canoe trip downriver next week," Bob Newall, the maintenance man, had told her that morning.

"So – I still don't get what this canoe trip is all about," Pim sighed between chews of her burger after they'd received their order at one of the indoor tables. Even inside, they'd had to pick up a telephone to talk to the kitchen, which Pim called "a marvel of 20th century efficiency."

Hester was only slightly taken aback when their food arrived on a model railroad car that followed tracks all over the restaurant.

"I think the canoe trip is another horrible idea from Candy Carmichael in Human Resources," Hester responded, using her napkin to wipe creamy mayonnaise from her mouth. "Candy was the one who led the whole 'Seven Habits' movement in the library a few years back, when we all had to come up with five 'win-win' ideas a week in each department. Remember when Reg Doolittle brought a chainsaw in to work and cut down Candy's office door after he'd been told to 'sharpen his saw' one too many times? I've seen a few flameouts over the years, but he was a class act. For a while, people all over Portland talked about 'going librarian' instead of 'going postal.' "

Pim, chuckling with the remembrance, paused to dab at her shirt where mustard from her burger had dripped on a tiki god.

"So we're supposed to learn how to be team players by doing some sort of Outward Bounder exercise with canoes? Has anybody told cute Candy that we're not a football team?"

Hester shook her head as she poked a fork at her coleslaw.

"I agree, Pim, it sounds stupid, but I guess it's supposed to tie into the whole Rose Festival theme, following Lewis and Clark's path and all that. I'm just going to pretend it's a fun day off work and try to enjoy myself. And if Candy tries to make us sing 'Kumbaya,' we throw her in the river. Is it a pact?"

Pim gave a thumbs up as she gobbled the last of her fries and they rose to return to the bookmobile.

"Let's see if there's any more news about the Rose Medallion," Pim said as she climbed into her seat and pulled out her transistor radio, just like one Hester had used to listen to Beatles songs when she was 7.

A patron who ran an antique store had offered Pim good money for the old radio, pointing out that she could use the cash to get a nice new Walkman. "Naw, that would have too many twiddly knobs and things, and this good old radio still works fine," responded Pim, whom Hester often called "a loyal Luddite of the first order."

Pim also vowed to drive her 1977 Gremlin until it qualified for classic plates.

Pim thumbed the tiny tuning wheel and the sound of KSNZ news radio squawked from the little speaker just in time for a news report.

"This is Misty Day, with a dramatic development in the Pieter van Dyke murder investigation. Portland Police Bureau, in cooperation with the Washington County Sheriff's Office, is holding what they call a 'person of interest' for questioning in the ritualistic killing of one of Portland's most prominent civic leaders. Jean Baptiste 'Pomp' Charbonneau VI, a printer for *The Oregonian* and reportedly a direct descendant of a member of the Lewis and Clark expedition, is being held so far only on a charge of reckless endangerment following an incident when he fled police from his trailer home in rural Washington County this morning. More details as they are available."

Pim, her jaw hanging open, clicked off the radio.

"Hester, they've arrested my friend Pomp. How screwed up can they get things? Pomp wouldn't hurt anybody!"

Her eyes shifted back and forth, then widened in realization. She turned to her colleague.

"This sounds like your buddy the inspector, all over again! Can't he get anything right?"

Hester, stunned that the murder investigation just wouldn't leave her alone, felt her heart sink.

"I don't know, Pim. I just don't know."

Chapter Eighteen

S ome of the week's worries faded on Saturday as Hester and Pim took the bookmobile on their monthly run up into the lovely Columbia River Gorge National Scenic Area.

It was another blazing, blue-sky day. As the big bus rounded the 700-foot promontory of Crown Point on the gorge's winding, historic highway, Hester could look down and see caravans of summer revelers turning off the freeway far below on their way to the beach at Rooster Rock State Park.

"We'll take this bend a little carefully," Pim said, as if to herself, the only acknowledgment they made of the previous bookmobile's demise when Hester had watched a confessed murderer drive it off this cliff.

That evening, Hester admitted she was actually kind of looking forward to the Macarena Cruise when Karen picked her up at 6.

The day had topped out at 86 degrees, and an open boat deck on the river might at least offer a cooler evening than she'd spend cooped up in her hot apartment with a fuzzy cat on her lap. And the promise of piña coladas didn't hurt.

At Hester's urging, Karen had extended the invitation to Linda Dimple, the children's librarian at Grand Central Library. Privately, Hester didn't think Linda spent enough time with adults. She secretly also thought Linda's wholesome presence might be a welcome dampener to Karen's matchmaking ambitions that evening.

"Oh, this is an excellent opportunity for me, the kids just love that dance and I've been wanting to do some research on it!" Linda trilled from the back seat of Karen's big BMW. "People often don't recognize the academic side of being a children's librarian. In grad school, I once wrote an entire term paper on the color blue!"

A half-hour later, as the big stern-wheeler, the Portland Rose, pushed off into the Willamette River from the dock at Gov. Tom McCall Waterfront Park, Hester and Linda leaned on a varnished teak railing together looking at the skyline while Karen went off in search of their first round of cocktails. Hester had changed into another favorite sundress, this one bedecked in pink cabbage roses. Linda wore a navy-blue sailor dress.

"I didn't know they made them in adult sizes," Karen had whispered cattily as she and Hester had walked up the gangplank behind Linda.

As the vessel blew its steam whistle, Linda waved wildly at the joggers and dog-walkers on shore.

"Farewell, farewell, we'll send a postcard from Southampton!" she shouted, pulling a handful of rolled confetti paper streamers from her pocket and unleashing them over the side.

To Hester's look of mild shock, Linda turned and explained, "I've never been on a cruise before! I wanted to do it right!"

At that moment Karen returned with three drinks squeezed together in her hands. As usual, Hester's childhood friend had dressed for the occasion – or, some might say, overdressed. For the warm evening, she wore snug-fitting Capri pants in a red, green and yellow floral print, a fire-engine red tank top and a necklace of lacquered, nearly life-size papier-mâché fruit.

"Shouldn't that fruit be on a hat, Carmen?" Hester said dryly.

Karen scrunched her button nose in a look Hester remembered well from grade school. "The night is still young!" she replied saucily.

"Speaking of fruit, I've never had a drink like this!" squeaked Linda, as Karen handed each of them a giant tulip glass with a large spear of pineapple and half a banana poking from a golden, frosty froth.

"Well don't be shy, because Teri June Inc. got us the all-drinks-included tickets, and my accountant says I can write it off as an entertainment expense because both of you help me so often in my book research!"

"Just be careful you don't put an eye out," Hester admonished, twisting her head sideways to dodge the pineapple spear and get her mouth on the fat red straw.

"Not so fast, ladies!" Karen interrupted, raising her glass to the golden sun that was just lowering to the top of the forested hills behind the city. "First, a toast."

The others raised their glasses as Karen continued.

"To Almost Summer, because it's just a week away, and we had one of the wettest winters ever seen."

"Hear, hear," Hester chimed in.

"To being back home in the sweetest little town around, because I've sampled plenty of others lately!" Karen hung her tongue and made a face of pinched exhaustion.

"And to dancing the night away!" she concluded with a shimmy of her ample hips.

They clinked glasses and took big sips.

A thoughtful look crossed Karen's face as she took a second slurp, swirled it between her teeth and then winced.

"The thing with these fruity, frosty drinks – First, they put hardly any liquor in them, because you can't taste it anyway. And second, they count on the fact that you get such an ice-cream headache you'll never be able to drink many!"

"Oh, I know how to counteract that!" Linda piped up. "My brother did a research paper on it in medical school. The trick is to rub your tongue on the roof of your mouth and warm your palate. It's a proven medical cure!"

For a moment all three women took on the look of preoccupied bullfrogs as they busily worked their tongues.

"Well, at least it gives you something to do, *and* makes sure that people stay away from you because you look like an idiot!" Hester quipped.

"Humph!" Karen responded. "Don't take that attitude, Hester dear. Tonight we're going to find you a man!"

At that moment an emcee with an overamplified microphone began to introduce the entertainers and Karen turned toward the stage. Hester made a face behind her back.

From there, the evening became a long blur in Hester's mind: of pink and orange sky reflected in the river; of the boat passing beneath what seemed like a dozen bridges, the lowest of which had to raise for the sternwheeler's tall black smokestacks; of seeing curious Portlanders climb from their idling cars to look down and laugh as the vessel passed beneath them. Hester wasn't sure they were always laughing "with" the dancing cruise-goers with outstretched arms windmilling in the air.

And throughout it all, endless repetitions of the signature "Macarena" song, played at evermore deafening decibels. Apparently the band hired for the cruise didn't know any other tunes.

Karen managed to cajole Hester into trying the dance a few times. Hester finally found a large potted palm to hide behind to escape the advances of a Bert Parks-lookalike with a terrible cheap toupee that showed baseball stitching up the part.

She was peeking through the palm fronds when she heard someone clear their throat. She looked around to see one of the wait staff offering her a tray with miniature tubs of guacamole and chips. Hester smiled wanly and shook her head at the curly-haired young man with two pierced nostrils.

Only after he'd stepped away did she remember him as one of the Rajneeshees who hung out on 23rd Avenue and regularly urged her to donate a dollar for a "free" flower. Was the murder case trying to edge back into her brain?

But that wasn't the big surprise of the evening.

Taking Karen's encouragement to heart, Linda Dimple hadn't been shy about keeping her glass topped up.

"No scurvy on this voyage!" she had announced with glee around 9 p.m. as she chewed on her 12th spear of pineapple for the night and stepped up to lead a conga line. While the band was on a break, recorded salsa music trumpeted from the loudspeakers.

Hester closed her eyes, fearing for Linda's head in the morning, and knowing that Sunday was one of the busier days for the children's room.

But suddenly Hester's eyes popped back open, as what she had just seen registered more clearly in her own slightly rum-addled brain.

The man in the conga line just behind Linda. The bald man with his hands firmly planted on the waggling hips of Grand Central Library's children's librarian. Didn't she know him?

Hester's hand flew to her lips as she stifled a slight burp. The buffet's enchiladas hadn't agreed with her, and a slight sour taste filled her mouth.

A taste not unlike sauerkraut.

Her hand pressed her lips even harder at the sudden recognition. Wearing an open-collared cotton shirt in an exotic Indonesian batik design above a pair of well-filled khaki Dockers, he was dressed differently than she'd seen before.

But the broadly smiling man behind Linda Dimple was Gerhard Gerbils.

"You sure weren't in mourning for long, Herr Wiener Dog," Hester whispered.

Chapter Nineteen

In staring at the dancers, Hester had inadvertently caught Linda's attention. Sometime in the evening's revelries, Hester noted with mild alarm, her diminutive colleague had topped off her sailor outfit with an oversize sombrero embroidered with, "Hola, my name is Jorge."

Linda veered the conga line over to Hester's potted palm and refused to continue until Hester joined them, cutting in a few people behind the Wiener Dog proprietor.

Another jolt came when Hester realized she recognized the wavy-haired, twenty-something young man, his biceps bulging the sleeves of a salmon-pink polo shirt, whose trim waist she now gripped.

"Say, didn't I see you on TV?" she shouted into his ear. "Didn't you find the Rose Medallion?"

He turned his flushed face back to her and smiled with perfect white teeth. "Yes! We're celebrating tonight!"

At that moment, the conga line was passing a cocktail table where Karen White was doing her best to fend off Bert Parks. Spying Hester and the young hunk exchanging words, Karen caught Hester's eye and gave her two enthusiastic thumbs up and a suggestive leer. Hester stuck out her tongue in reply.

After the conga line had finally broken up and the dancers had descended on the buffet now filled with a fresh assortment of Latin-inspired desserts, a curious Hester noticed that her buff dance partner and the nubile young blonde who had been ahead of him in the lineup had joined Gerbils and a knot of others, many of whom looked like family.

Hester grabbed a spoon and a small flan garnished with strawberries and quickly found a seat at an adjoining table facing away from the group, with a view of the churning paddlewheel at the stern of the ship.

A loud pop of a cork and a cry of "Cava!" told her that Gerbils and his family weren't ready to stop celebrating just yet.

At the sound of "tinga, tinga, tinga" as someone behind her tapped a spoon against a glass to silence the group, Hester cocked an ear that way.

When the happy chatter around the table had ceased, it was the Wiener Dog proprietor who spoke.

"I want to once again congratulate young Tony, our talented chef, on his good fortune this week. And besides his happy plans which most of you already know – to wed our lovely Greta next month – I have some more wonderful news!"

Gerbils' booming baritone voice dripped with bonhomie and familial spirit, inspired by more than a few piña coladas, Hester guessed.

"I want our family and friends to be the first to know that I have offered, and Tony has enthusiastically accepted, a partnership in Wiener Dog Incorporated!"

Happy cries, a smattering of applause and the clink of glasses ensued, along with words of congratulation. The chatter resumed at full volume, just as the sternwheeler's haunting whistle announced they were arriving back at the dock.

"Hmmm," Hester wondered to herself as she gobbled a final strawberry and plopped her spoon down, ready to track down her friends and call it a night. "I wonder just how much of that $50,000 young Mr. Biceps will ever see!"

Chapter Twenty

Nate Darrow had spent long hours the previous afternoon interviewing Pomp Charbonneau in the Washington County Jail in Hillsboro, just west of Portland.

Unless and until Portland filed a murder charge that would take precedence over the reckless endangerment and property damage charges on which Wayne Jordan arrested him, protocol dictated that Charbonneau would remain in the Hillsboro lockup.

So far, the winemaker hadn't fessed up to much. To Darrow's relief, a bail hearing was delayed until Monday afternoon.

Saturday, Darrow welcomed the sunny weather as he'd headed north to Vancouver Lake, tucked inside a bend of the Columbia, where he'd taken the first in a series of windsurfing lessons for which he'd signed up.

That afternoon he'd taken Sven in for some service at the local Volvo mechanic, then picked up some supplies from the do-it-yourself brewer's warehouse and went back to the Luxor to run a load of wash. In the laundry room, he spent 20 minutes fending off the attentions of Mrs. Kleinholtz from 419, who wanted to debate whether Glock or Smith & Wesson made the better police revolver.

He'd planned a quiet night with some Thai takeout and an old favorite video. It was after 10 p.m. and Darrow was on his third beer when someone buzzed at his door.

Like many apartments in the Pacific Northwest, the Luxor had no air conditioning. And Darrow had swung the door wide before he remembered he'd stripped down to just his sheerest nylon running shorts to try to beat the heat.

"Oh!" Hester exclaimed, her eyes doing a quick up and down of his lean frame before she stopped to stare at the floor.

"Oh," Darrow said, holding a forefinger up to ask her to wait while he ducked back into the recesses of his apartment. In a moment, he reappeared wrapped in a white terry robe.

Hester declined his offer of beer but gratefully accepted an iced tea, then sat at her neighbor's old pastel green Formica kitchen table as she told Darrow of her strange encounters aboard the Portland Rose earlier in the evening.

"First the Rajneeshee waiter, then Gerbils and his son-in-law-to-be and a whole gaggle of happy family – I kept looking underfoot for Schnitzel the Wonder Dog!"

Darrow, in a beery haze, looked as if he was digesting the story and about to say something profound, but instead stifled a small hiccup and announced, "In third grade we had a gerbil in our classroom – you know, one of those little ratty, hamster kind of animals? And we took turns taking it home for the weekend, to take care of it. Name was Cindy. But when I took it home, it escaped from its little cage somehow. For months, my mother kept finding little nests of shredded newspaper in the back of closets, but we never did find Cindy."

He concluded with a tiny burp and a melancholy smile.

Hester rolled her eyes. "Has anybody ever told you you're a big help?"

He looked at her with watery eyes and offered a bowl of pretzels from which he'd been snacking. Hester, shaking her head, rose and gathered empty takeout cartons from the table, tossed them in a trash bin under the sink and grabbed a wet sponge to wipe a puddle of congealed peanut sauce from the table.

"You know that we picked up Charbonneau, right?" Darrow asked, hoisting his now-warm third beer and rocking back on two legs of the kitchen chair. "Dumb bastard made a royal mess of a nice vineyard out in the West Valley."

He paused to sip at the beer as Hester, spying a lemon in a fruit bowl on the counter, grabbed a knife and cut a slice to squeeze into her iced tea.

"Well, he admits he printed the faked postage-stamp and envelope, but he says he was hired to do it by Pieter van Dyke, who wanted a replica of his father's most-prized possession. For sentimental reasons."

Hester, swirling the ice cubes in her tea, tried not to peer at Darrow's curly brown chest hairs, clearly visible where his robe was now gaping open. From the living room TV, she could hear muffled snatches of Walter Matthau and Glenda Jackson chatting in an old spy caper that Darrow hadn't turned off. On the kitchen counter, a small electric fan rotated on its stand with a redundant clicking and whirring that stirred the air briefly every time it turned her way.

Nate, finding solace in venting his frustrations, wasn't finished.

"The heck of it is that by putting his great-granddaddy in the canoe and signing his own name, he probably skates around a counterfeiting charge because the law applies only if you make a copy that can't be readily told apart from the real thing," Nate said with a chuckle of grudging admiration.

Hester sighed and shook her head. "And even Eldon Purdy, my most annoying library patron, declared it a laughable fake!"

They shared ironic smiles. Then another thought crossed Hester's face.

"But if he made the replica as a keepsake for Pieter, what was the copy doing in the McLoughlin Collection? There's no denying that a collector's item potentially worth a small fortune is missing!"

Darrow cocked his forefinger at her like he was firing a pistol. "Exactly, Miss Marple!"

Hester gave him her best scowl and backhanded Darrow on the shoulder as he did a grinning duck and cover. Jumping from his chair, pouring the warm beer into the sink, then grabbing a cold one from the fridge and popping the cap in one swift move, he elaborated.

"Get this. Our Francophile friend claims van Dyke was the scheming crook in the whole affair. He tells a cockamamie story about how the library president had sold the real first-day cover to a deep-pockets Japanese collector, banked the money and just wanted the copy as a substitute in the library collection."

Hester gasped at the suggestion. "Oh, dear, does he have any way to prove that?"

"Well, we're looking at van Dyke's bank records, but if it's true and he had any sense at all it probably went to someplace in the Cayman Islands where they aren't too fussy about reporting to the IRS."

"Oh – what about the whole thing with the French pistol?" Hester interjected.

"That I haven't worn him down on yet. He's trying to play it innocent. I thought I'd give him today to stew about it and then drop in on him tomorrow for another chat, and I'm taking my thumbscrews." He gave a diabolical leer.

"It's a shame you have to work on a Sunday, Mr. de Sade, and with the weather so lovely," Hester riposted.

She paused in thought for a moment, then continued with a shy grin.

"If you have to spend the day at the salt mines, why don't you give yourself a break in the evening and have dinner at my place. I'm making chicken curry – nice and spicy; it's a strangely satisfying thing for a hot day. And I like to do a giant platter of chilled watermelon, fresh pineapple and kiwi fruit on the side. It's the perfect complement."

Darrow gave her a long and appreciative gaze, then self-consciously pulled his robe tighter.

"That sounds like a wonderful way to end a long day after slaving over medieval torture devices, Ms. McGarrigle. Count me in."

Chapter Twenty-one

Sunday, June 16

Sunday dawned without a cloud. A laser-like sunbeam streaming through a crack in the bedroom curtains awakened Hester early. She took a moment to come out of a dream in which she'd been swimming in Diamond Lake, up in the Cascade Mountains, where her family used to vacation. In her dream, she'd gotten a stitch in her side and was sinking into the water, with pressure building and building in her chest. It wasn't pleasant but somehow it wasn't frightening because in her dream she somehow knew she could wake up and it would just be a dream.

Her eyes popped open.

"Oh, it's you. I should have known."

Bingle T. was perched high on Hester's chest, his big green eyes gazing unblinkingly into hers. Somehow, it seemed, he could will her awake. And the weight of the big Maine Coon had given her the drowning dream more than once.

The cat made no sound but calmly reached out a tufted paw and gently poked Hester's forehead.

"Yes, it's after dawn so it must be breakfast time, I know how you think, fishbreath," she murmured.

Slipping out from under the puffy white comforter that was her only bedding in the summer months and pulling on her fuzzy pink slippers, Hester parted the chrysanthemum-print curtains and sucked in a breath at the morning's brilliance. She pushed the window wider and took a deep lungful of the sweet morning air.

No cars yet buzzed up Everett Street. The only sound was the call of a sparrow in one of the big-leaf maples lining the street and the cheerful ring of a bicycle bell. Hester looked down and waved as Mr. Manicotti from Apartment 302 pushed his old three-wheeled Schwinn out to the sidewalk and pedaled off toward a favorite coffee shop.

"This is it!" Hester exclaimed, turning back to Bingle T. "It's Rose Garden Breakfast Day!"

Hester's mother had started the tradition years ago as a mother-daughter outing that had turned into a happy annual event. Once school was out, they'd wait for the first cloudless June day and take a breakfast picnic up the hill to Portland's famous International Rose Test Garden in Washington Park.

They'd get there early, long before the crowds, spread a blanket and have the garden all to themselves, with the roses at peak bloom scenting the morning air with every imaginable variation of sweet aroma.

Now that her parents had retired to a comfy cottage on the Oregon Coast, Hester occasionally invited a friend. But spontaneity was part of the pleasure, so usually she just took Bingle T.

It was barely 8 a.m. when she parked in an empty hillside lot and looked out with pleasure over the sprawling rows of flowering rose bushes and the view beyond of the city skyline and snowy Mount Hood.

Bingle T. appeared out from under a seat, where he usually hid while the car was in motion. Hester clipped a line on to the small dog harness the big cat wore for such outings, though Hester never used the "d" word when squeezing him into it.

Wearing some old black jeans and a favorite T-shirt, she gathered up her wicker picnic basket, stocked with a Thermos of coffee, a fresh orange, slices of Granny Smith apple, and the main course: a footlong maple bar she'd picked from the bakery case at Rose's, a 23rd Avenue legend specializing in Paul Bunyan-sized baked goods. As the *Oregonian's* food critic had once put it, a shipment of Rose's cinnamon rolls could "solve the problem of Third World hunger in one swell foop."

"I don't know about foops, but the baked goods *are* pretty swell," Hester told Bingle T. as she broke off a corner of maple-glazed pastry and dunked it in coffee.

From answering questions on Reference Line, Hester knew that Portland's fascination with roses reached back to the highbrow tastes of the city's upper classes in the 1890s. By 1905, Portland had 200 miles of rose-bordered city streets, which helped attract visitors to the Lewis and Clark Centennial celebration that year. Washington Park's rose garden originated with a World War I effort to save the finest strains of hybrid roses grown in Europe lest they be lost in the bombing.

As was tradition, Hester had spread her blanket on the grass next to a planting of the current year's All-America Rose Selections. For 1996, that included, appropriately, a rose named Mount Hood – a grandiflora that sprawled like a snowdrift of perfect, cone-shaped white blooms.

Bingle T. didn't particularly like being on a leash. He usually did his best to discourage Hester from taking him on what she called "walkies" by constantly wrapping his line around fence posts, parking meters, or, in this case, rose bushes. On one memorable outing to a park that had peacocks, a peacock's sudden bugling call sent the big cat rocketing 15 feet up a Douglas fir until he reached the end of his leash. Hester had no alternative but to yank him back down, inch by inch, as if she was hauling in a boat anchor. The term "like herding cats" held a special poignancy for her.

But her feline companion, his leash tied to a nearby stair railing, had now settled down under a planting of crimson-red Chrysler Imperial, the All-America Rose of 1953. He alternately nibbled grass and chewed on his own special breakfast of Kitty Snax while Hester sipped her coffee and pondered the mystery of Pieter van Dyke.

Did his murder really have something to do with shady dealings at the library? The business with the faked first-day cover sounded awfully fishy. And the fact that the murder weapon was a replica of a pistol owned by this Charbonneau character didn't do anything to steer suspicion away from him.

Hester also realized that if the pistol replica had been kept at Fort Vancouver, Charbonneau might easily have had access to it – and, unlike many people, would have known how to use it.

"But why use a weapon that would so easily point to him?" she asked her furry breakfast partner, pausing only to yank him away from digging under an orange hybrid tea rose called – coincidentally – Bing Crosby (All-America Rose, 1981).

As she watched a jet contrail tracking into the blue sky from the direction of Portland International Airport, Hester's wandering mind also flashed back to Dabney Pensler's stress attack that had conveniently sent him home when the first-day cover fraud was discovered. Nobody had better access to the McLoughlin Collection. Could the fussy pince nez conceal the face of a criminal?

Pausing from her breakfast, Hester dug into her bag for the old Pentax Spotmatic that used to be her father's favorite camera. Over the years, roses at their peak of bloom had become one of Hester's sentimental favorite photo subjects. She'd shoot the flowers in black-and-white, make prints at the public lab at Portland State University and then hand-color them, giving an arty 1920s look. They would be cards and framed gifts to friends and family through the year. Her mother kept prodding her to stage a gallery show.

As she happily focused and snapped her way along a row, her mind kept mulling the mystery.

There's the whole question of the weird ritualistic way van Dyke was killed. Was there really some cult involved?

"It sure seems like the Rajneeshees keep cropping up!" she said aloud, her cheeks pinking when she realized she'd caught the attention of an early-rising pair of octogenarians who now peered at her over a nearby row of coppery-orange blossoms called Singin' in the Rain (1995).

"Come along, Horace, it's when they start talking to themselves that they become dangerous," said the sweater-wrapped female half of the duo, whose blue-rinsed pincurls closely matched a lavender-hued floribunda behind her.

But was there really a ritual involved here, Hester wondered? Maybe someone just held a terrible grudge against van Dyke and didn't just want him dead but wanted him dead *and* humiliated. Staking out a pasty, somewhat potbellied middle-aged man in a spread-eagled pose in his underpants was certainly humiliating.

Or maybe it wasn't just a humiliating pose. Hester's mind reeled as she thought back to her Art History classes at the University of Washington, where one of her professors was a Leonardo da Vinci nut. What if Pieter van Dyke had been posed like Leonardo's Vitruvian Man, in some strange message only a master of symbology might understand?

"No, that sounds too much like the plot of a bad novel where the answer can be found only by holding 'The Last Supper' up to a mirror and counting the disciples," Hester admitted sheepishly to herself.

As she put away her camera, Hester realized that she hoped, somehow, the murderer wasn't Pim's friend Charbonneau. She felt an inexplicable need for Pim to forgive Nate Darrow.

"Why do people always feel the need for one friend to like another friend?" she groaned aloud, turning just in time to see Lavender Pincurls looking owlishly back her way while poking her finger in Horace's back to prod him to move faster toward their Buick in the nearby lot.

Of course, there was also the strange coincidence about the Rose Medallion being found by someone linked to one of Pieter van Dyke's law partners. And was there really anything to learn from the medallion, evidence-wise? She made a mental note to quiz Nate Darrow about that.

Also not to be forgotten was Gerhard Gerbils' mysterious admonishment to Darrow at the Wiener Dog. Did van Dyke have any enemies who were recently released from prison?

Too many questions. And too big a maple bar. Hester wrapped up the leftovers, stashed everything in her picnic basket, untied her cat and headed for home.

Chapter Twenty-two

Harry Harrington and his wife had just left the old stone St. James Lutheran Church on the leafy downtown park blocks when the pocket of Harry's green herringbone suit started burbling.

"Hang on a second, Harriet, it's that doggone new gizmo," Harry said to his spouse, a sallow-faced, 54-year-old, 100-pound CPA whose wheat-colored hair hid in a pillbox hat above her pumpkin-colored linen blazer and skirt. The pair had met at a Willamette University sorority party 30 years earlier and thought the combination of their names was so funny they had no choice but to wed.

Harrington finally wrestled the phone from his pocket and hit the button to answer.

Harry wasn't adept with the new phone. Besides the IBM Selectric typewriter he still used to write reports, his closest brush with anything "high-tech" was during his days of using a walkie-talkie in the Navy. So whenever he spoke into the new phone he held it out in front of him and spoke loudly, with careful enunciation.

"YES, NATE, WHAT IS IT?"

"Listen, Harry, sorry to bug you on Sunday, I know you're probably only just getting out of church, but there's a loose end we need to follow on van Dyke."

"WELL, NATE, LIKE MY MOTHER ALWAYS USED TO SAY, 'SORRY DOESN'T BUTTER THE PARSNIPS!' BUT WHAT DO YOU NEED, BUDDY?"

"I'm heading out to Hillsboro to interview that Charbonneau clown again, but I wonder if you could check if there might be anybody who van Dyke or his family made an enemy of, in their legal profession, who got sent to prison and maybe just got released."

Harrington, having listened with the phone pressed to his ear, again held it out in front of him.

"OH, I GET IT, NATE, YOU'RE THINKING SOME EX-CON MIGHT HAVE HAD A MOTIVE TO OFF VAN DYKE?"

"Well, you never know. Maybe a check of prison release records…"

"I DON'T HAVE TO CHECK PRISON RECORDS, I CAN TELL YOU OFF THE TOP OF MY HEAD. YOU GOTTA REMEMBER, YOU'RE WORKING WITH A GUY WHO'S BEEN AROUND THIS TOWN A WHILE. AND IT HAPPENS I READ IN THE PAPER THAT ONE OF THE HEAD RAJNEESHEES INVOLVED IN THAT SALAD BAR POISONING, MA ANAND CARLA, GOT OUT TWO WEEKS AGO."

"Yeah? Well, I'm sure that got our chief all hot and bothered, but what does that have to do with van Dyke?"

"WELL YOU MIGHT ASK, WHAT DOES THAT HAVE TO DO WITH VAN DYKE?" Harrington smirked. He loved to show off his near-encyclopedic knowledge of the Oregon legal system, which Nate was quickly learning to value.

"Yes, Harry." Darrow put on his patient voice. "I did ask."

"WELL, NATE, IT SO HAPPENS HER APPEAL WAS ONE OF THE LAST CASES THAT WENT BEFORE OLD JUDGE VAN DYKE, PIETER'S GRANDFATHER, BEFORE HE RETIRED FROM THE SUPREME COURT IN SALEM. HE SPOKE OUT STRONGLY FOR CONVICTION AND WAS PRETTY MUCH CREDITED FOR SEEING SHE GOT LOCKED UP FOR 10 YEARS. HER 10 YEARS WERE UP LAST WEEK."

The phone line was silent as Darrow took this in.

"OK, well that's a connection, I'd say. But how likely is it that she'd hold that big a grudge against the judge's grandson?"

"WELL, MAYBE YOU DIDN'T FOLLOW THE RAJNEESHEE STORY AS CLOSELY AS I DID, BUT YOU NEED TO KNOW THAT MA ANAND CARLA WAS MORE LOOP-DE-LOO THAN ANY OF THEM, AND BOY DID SHE HAVE A MOUTH ON HER. WHEN THE OLD MAN READ HIS JUDGMENT SHE GOT UP IN COURT AND

SAID – AND I QUOTE – 'I WILL COME BACK AND FUDGE UP YOUR LIFE, MISTER, AND I WILL FUDGE UP YOUR CHILDREN'S LIVES, AND YOUR CHILDREN'S CHILDREN!' ONLY THING IS, NATE? SHE DIDN'T SAY 'FUDGE.' "

Again, Darrow brooded silently for a moment.

"Rajneeshees again. I just don't believe this," he said, adding a word that also wasn't fudge. "How did we miss this connection earlier? The chief will skin us if this has anything to do with van Dyke's murder."

By now, Harriet Harrington was plucking at Harry's sleeve and pointing to her watch to remind him they had a date for mimosas with the pastor and his wife. Harry was glad he had an excuse to beg off. The pastor's wife always used the cheapest frozen orange juice in her mimosas. Harry claimed it was made using nothing but pits and peels.

"YEAH, NATE, I THINK THE CHIEF WILL BE HOT ON THIS RAJNEESHEE CONNECTION AGAIN. LET ME SEE IF I CAN TRACK HER DOWN."

"OK, Harry, why don't you make a few phone calls to old friends and neighbors, but keep it on the sly. If that doesn't lead anywhere we'll take a run out to Sauvie Island first thing tomorrow, just to be sure she hasn't shown up there. Right now I'm psyched up and loaded for bear to go to work on Charbonneau. With his link to the pistol I still see him as our best suspect."

"OK, LOADED FOR BEAR, I HEAR YOU. SAUVIE ISLAND FIRST THING TOMORROW. ROGER THAT, NATE."

As Harrington punched the disconnect button and dropped the phone into his pocket, another member of the St. James congregation, standing behind an oak tree a few feet away, pulled her phone out of her purse and punched a quick-dial button.

"Yeah, Sid? Listen, it's Misty. I need a satellite van first thing tomorrow for Sauvie Island. And book me with a live feed for the morning news. I've got a break on the van Dyke case."

Chapter Twenty-three

As he drove toward the Washington County Jail in Hillsboro, Darrow remembered another phone call he needed to make. He was in a sour mood, driving a boxy old brown Volvo station wagon on loan from Orvald, his cranky Swedish auto repairman. He'd had to leave Sven at the garage again – something about tie rods that sounded expensive.

Steering with his knees and holding the cellphone even with the dashboard so he could more or less watch the road, he managed to punch the number for the Police Bureau's lab.

The phone buzzed six times before being answered by a youthful voice that Nate recognized as James Chin, a twenty-something whiz kid who ran the lab on Sundays.

"Hey, Jimmy, it's Nate Darrow, calling to see if you have anything yet on the Rose Medallion."

An ear-rattling slurping sound indicated that the bristle-haired science geek was in his usual pose, with his red Converse All Stars up on a desk while sucking Mountain Dew through a straw from a Big Gulp cup.

"Oh, sure, they filed the report late last night, I was going to give you a buzz. Hang on."

Nate heard the phone drop, followed by a solid minute of shuffling noises and the sound of a tinny radio being tuned to a rap station before Chin picked up again.

"Yeah, here it is. The only fingerprints were from the medallion's finder, Anthony Pucci, 28, of Gresham. There was some dog hair – no surprise there, I understand. Traces of what we think is squirrel dung. We didn't have a confirmed sample to authenticate by, but if you want me to run over to the Park Blocks I could probably remedy that. Oh, and get this:

sausage grease. Quite a bit of it in the fine grooves of the medallion's detailing."

Darrow's knee jerked and he dropped the phone as he grabbed for the steering wheel to keep the wagon from veering into an 18-wheeler next to him on the Sunset Highway.

After ducking to the floor to retrieve the phone and getting an airhorn blast from the truck in the next lane, he responded to Chin.

"Tell me more about that last thing. Did you say sausage grease?"

More pages flipping, another slurp and the sound of chopsticks scraping a takeout carton as Chin finished last night's leftover chicken chow yuk from Hung Far Low, one of Portland's oldest Chinese restaurants.

"Umm, yeah, there was pork and beef fat mingled with spices typical of, like, German sausage or bratwurst, says here."

"Do me a favor and check the chain of evidence. Wasn't that medallion turned in to officers on the scene at Forest Park? The finder didn't take it anywhere else, right?"

"Uh, let's see. Nope, nowhere else. Officers took custody of the medallion at the park and gave the finder a receipt on-site."

Darrow's eyes bounced from his rearview mirror to his speedometer and back to the road as his mind worked.

"And you say the grease was worked into the crevices on the medallion? Not something that would have just happened from being casually handled by someone who worked in a kitchen?"

"Well, you might need to check that with Don Finkle, who wrote the report, but his notes here indicate the amount of grease in the grooves of the medallion's design – like the lines that make up the rose image – was consistent with the whole medal being rubbed with, or even dipped in, grease."

Darrow didn't hesitate to respond this time.

"Jimmy, if I brought you a sausage from the right restaurant, could that grease be matched to its source?"

"Ummm, yeah, I think it probably could be. We could even do DNA analysis on the pork and beef that could be a real lock if you needed."

Darrow thanked him and punched the disconnect button just as he took the exit at Hillsboro, then pulled the wagon to the shoulder and hit quick-dial for another number.

"Hey, Harry, it's me again."

"NATE, LONG TIME NO HEAR!"

"Look, Harry, I know this is messing up your plans for the day, but I wonder if you and Harriet like German food, 'cause I gotta ask another favor. When you're done checking out the rabid Rajneeshee lady, could you maybe take your wife to lunch at the Wiener Dog, out at Jantzen Beach? Enjoy your meal, but also say you're having a party later and want an order of every sausage they make, packed to go. And take it straight to Jimmy Chin in the lab. He'll be expecting you."

"HOT DOGS FOR SUNDAY BRUNCH? I DON'T KNOW HOW WELL THAT WILL PLAY WITH HARRIET!"

"Talk up sauerbraten and spätzle, but be sure and get takeout of every sausage and bratwurst on the menu. I have a hunch I can tell you about later, but if you do this and it pays off I'll buy beer on Fridays for a month."

"OK, NATE, I LIKE THOSE ODDS."

"And Harry? Don't let on you're a cop, just act hungry."

Chapter Twenty-four

Hester had spent the afternoon doing some laundry and packing for the next day's trip on the Columbia River.

She was finally sipping a glass of good Dundee pinot gris in her cozy little yellow kitchen as she stirred a bubbling pot of golden curry sauce and watched the baby carrots swim among islands of Yukon Gold potato. Cooking good food – especially comfort food her mother taught her to make – always made her hum happily.

Every time she opened the fridge she stole another peek at dessert: a tray of cream puffs she'd concocted in between washing loads. She'd carefully drizzled the crusty tops with the just-right thin icing made from bittersweet baker's chocolate, as prescribed in the recipe from her grandmother's homemade cookbook. This was the family dessert she'd grown up adoring.

"I remember the first time I got them just right," she told Bingle T. as he sat on her kitchen windowsill watching for hummingbirds at a new feeder hanging outside. "When I took a bite and they tasted just like Nana's, I got tears in my eyes."

Lost in thought, she took a sip of wine, then finished the memory.

"Of course I didn't get the proportions right, and each cream puff was the size of a human head, but they tasted great!" she said with a chuckle.

When the door buzzer sounded at 6:25 Hester quickly flipped on the rice cooker, stepped to the hallway mirror to push a steam-limped red curl back behind her ear and swung open the door to welcome Nate Darrow.

The evening was still warm, but on his return from Hillsboro Darrow had stopped back in his apartment for a cool shower and now presented himself in baggy, caramel-colored cotton slacks, Teva sport sandals and a burgundy polo shirt. He carried a small bouquet of purple irises and a bottle of wine.

Hester had changed into a blue batik butterfly top, somewhat resembling an old tablecloth with a hole for her head, over a pair of white culottes. Her bare feet showed off freshly polished crimson-red toenails.

Nate looked her up and down. "My, that's a more bohemian look than usual for the lady of this house." He paused. "It suits you, Hester."

She batted her eyelashes exaggeratedly, smiled and led him to her cheerful kitchen and a wicker chair at a round, two-seater pedestal table next to a pair of open windows. The table held two place settings on mats of red linen.

"We're dining at the Round Table tonight, Sir Nathaniel of Everett Street, because this lovely southeasterly breeze kicked in a half-hour ago and it's rather heavenly with the windows thrown wide," she said. "I've got fans running in the rest of the apartment but they're just moving the hot air around."

"Ah, this is nice," Darrow said, laughing as a little freshet coming up from the river wrapped a gauzy curtain around his head.

"Oh, put this cookbook on the sill to hold those down. Bingle was perched there until he heard the buzzer. He usually goes into hiding until he's decided it's someone he likes."

The furry, gray-striped cat took that moment to stalk into the kitchen with his tail up like an exclamation point, leap onto Darrow's lap and then back to the windowsill, where he promptly settled into meatloaf position to look outside.

Surprise flashed across Hester's face. "Well! I guess you've passed muster, good knight. Cold beer or a drop of this nice wine?"

"I'll have what you're having, please."

As she pulled down another crystal goblet, one of two she'd brought home from a trip to Venice, Hester took the opportunity to ask Nate about his day – and how the case was going.

"Oh, God, I spent a hot afternoon in an airless little interrogation room with Gomer, I mean Pomp, Charbonneau."

He squeezed his palms against both temples and made a sound like a deflating tire.

"Anyway – our survivalist Gaul refused to lawyer up, protesting his innocence, but when it became apparent that we really did think he might have killed van Dyke, he spilled like milk. He now admits that he made van Dyke strip and staked him out in the horseshoe pit but insists he only did it to humiliate him because van Dyke had made a chump of him – Charbonneau – by cutting him out of the big payoff from the Japanese collector."

He took the wine glass from Hester and gave it a swirl and an appreciative sniff before continuing.

"Actually, it's hard to blame old Pomp for being a little ticked, since van Dyke seemed perfectly happy to let him take the blame for counterfeiting the Flying Canoe cover when all the time Charbonneau thought he was just making a collector's copy."

Darrow brooded for a moment, then decided to share more details with his neighbor, who'd proven she could be a discreet – and helpful – sounding board.

"Charbonneau says he called van Dyke and arranged a midnight meeting in the park, demanding that van Dyke share some of his newfound wealth. He wouldn't exactly own up to it but I gather old Pomp was dabbling in the ancient art of blackmail, something along the line of 'bring me 20,000 bucks or I'll tell my friends at the newspaper about your sleight of hand with library property.' He claims van Dyke showed up with the old pistol and no cash, hoping to scare Charbonneau off. But van Dyke stunk of gin, and it wasn't hard to take the gun away, Charbonneau says."

Hester sat down opposite Nate and set out a plate of butterfly crackers with runny brie topped by jalapeño jelly. She sipped at her wine and put her head back to compute what he was telling her.

"So maybe the pistol *had* been returned to the library from Fort Vancouver, and Pieter van Dyke borrowed it because it was an easy way to get a gun?" Hester posed.

Darrow tasted his wine for the first time as he thought back over the story and nodded.

"Out of curiosity, I made a quick call and van Dyke's wife claimed he never owned a gun. Hated them, and wouldn't know how to shoot one."

Hester took this in.

"So Charbonneau admits he was the shooter?"

"No. But of course he wouldn't, would he? He swears on the good name of Sacajawea – who I guess really is his great-great-grandmother or something – that van Dyke was alive when he left the park that night, and swearing a blue streak at him until his mouth was taped."

"What about the library pistol?" Hester asked, hopping up to stir the bubbling curry and then returning to the little table.

Darrow paused while he munched down a cracker, giving an appreciative "Mmmm, mmm" as he chewed.

"He says once van Dyke was trussed up, he left the old library pistol sitting on van Dyke's fat belly, unfired. He figured being caught with the purloined pistol would cook van Dyke's goose even if he didn't squeal on him."

Hester spread brie on a cracker and chewed it in thought. "But wait – what about the whole Rose Medallion connection? How did that play into it?"

Nate shook his head in mild wonder.

"Well, that's where I have to start wondering if Charbonneau might just be innocent – of murder, anyway. He says he wanted van Dyke to be humiliated and uncomfortable for a few hours but he *didn't* want the guy to be out there so long that he'd die of exposure. So, see, he works at *The Oregonian* and helps put together the page that gives the Rose Medallion clue every day. He knows that as the search goes on, the daily clues get more and more obvious about where the medallion is hidden, and this search was already only three days away from what they call 'the giveaway clue.' So he manages to switch clues for that next day, inserting the giveaway clue – something the contest coordinator at the newspaper confirmed for me, and is royally peeved about, by the way. Considering the fanatical legions that hunt for this thing, compounded by the big cash prize this time, Charbonneau says his clue switch virtually guaranteed that not only would someone find van Dyke within a half-hour of the first paper hitting the streets that next morning, but it ensured maximum exposure, if you'll pardon the term, of van Dyke's humiliation – which apparently Charbonneau planned to carry through with whether old Pieter brought the payoff or not."

"But hold on, what about the press breakdown?" Hester responded. "We were the first people to find van Dyke, and it was long after the normal time for the newspaper to come out. None of the medallion hunters got the clue in time."

"Right. Charboneau admits things didn't go as planned. But he says he had no way of knowing about the press breakdown when he left van Dyke; that's a part of the printing process that happens after he goes home. He claims it gave *someone* extra time to come across van Dyke and kill him. Charbonneau insists he left van Dyke by quarter to 1, and the medical examiner places the time of death at between 3 and 5 a.m. "

Thinking skeptically, Hester made a face as if she'd gotten a piece of bad cheese.

"But if the Rose Medallion was worth $50,000, why wouldn't Charbonneau have just taken it with him? Then he wouldn't have cared about any payoff from Pieter van Dyke!"

"Well, as an *Oregonian* employee, neither Charbonneau nor any of his relatives was eligible to claim the prize. He says he pulled the medallion off the park sign and left it on a ribbon around van Dyke's neck, just to make the humiliation complete."

"Wow," Hester sighed. "The whole thing sounds diabolical. And if it's true it certainly steers suspicion away from Charbonneau as the killer, unless he's one of those people who really wants to be caught. Maybe he *is* that weird?"

Darrow absently fingered the leaves of the irises Hester had put in a vase on the table, then spread brie on two crackers and munched them quickly down, his eyes momentarily popping wide when he got to the hot jelly. He sipped some cool wine, then spoke again.

"The thing is – he has an oddball sense of humor, but I have to say this guy doesn't feel like a liar to me, Hester. And I've listened to a few good liars in my day."

She put down her wineglass and hopped up to check on the steaming rice before responding.

"So if not Charbonneau, *who?*"

Darrow shrugged.

"I'm still noodling that. Got a few irons in the fire. In the meantime, Charbonneau's confession lets us hold him on obstruction, at least, and assault, maybe with intent. And we're moving him to our jail."

Chapter Twenty-five

The curry over jasmine rice was just as Hester promised: the perfect antidote to hot weather, and the fresh fruit on the side was like a culinary plunge into a cool forest stream.

With the cream puffs, they finished the bottle of unoaked, biodynamic chardonnay Nate had brought from his brother's winery. As the light began to fade, bells gonged from the Trinity Episcopal Cathedral, a Gothic-revival wonder just down the street.

Darrow held his glass aloft, struck an "I'm-going-to-quote-some-poetry-now" pose and then spoke in a soft and melodic baritone:

"The curfew tolls the knell of parting day,
The lowing herd winds slowly o'er the lea,
The plowman homeward plods his weary way,
And leaves the world to darkness and to me."

Hester arched an eyebrow.

"Really, not just named for Hawthorne but a reciter of Thomas Gray, Mr. Darrow? I'm impressed."

Darrow feigned a wounded look.

"I have more culture than you know, Ms. McGarrigle. And it happens my mother paid me $5 to memorize 'Elegy Written in a Country Churchyard' when I was 10 years old. The woman saw great things for her boys."

"Ah." She looked into his dark eyes and held the gaze. "I think I would have liked your mom."

Darrow held her eyes, then broke the moment by picking up the wine bottle and staring owlishly at the label.

"Winemakers call this naked chardonnay, when they don't put it on oak," Darrow said. "But it's one of the few things that I'm not sure is improved by being naked."

Hester turned slightly pink and swatted his hand, then took it and led him into the living room, pushing him toward the long sofa of faded chintz with big red roses. She stepped back into the kitchen for a few moments, then reappeared with a small plate of Stilton cheese and two tiny glasses of ruby port.

"Quote some more of 'Churchyard," Hester implored her neighbor. "Please."

Darrow gave her a puckish look. "Ah. You're going to challenge me."

He sat up straight and rolled his eyes upward in thought for a moment, then inserted his hand inside an imaginary vest in a Napoleonic pose and spoke again in the same lilting manner:

"Now fades the glimm'ring landscape on the sight,
And all the air a solemn stillness holds,
Save where the beetle wheels his droning flight,
And drowsy tinklings lull the distant folds."

Hester started to applaud, but Nate glared at her and she froze. He continued:

"Save that from yonder ivy-mantled tow'r
The moping owl does to the moon complain
Of such, as wand'ring near her secret bow'r,
Molest her ancient solitary reign."

This time Darrow stopped and bowed.

"And that old chestnut goes on for 32 stanzas – believe me, as one who once earned something like 15 cents a stanza, I've counted."

Hester's face shone with delight.

"I'd love to hear it all sometime. I love to read good poetry, but the only thing I've ever had a head for memorizing was 'The Cremation of Sam McGee.' I recited it in Fourth Grade."

Darrow's face lit up.

"Robert Service! Now *there's* an artist!" He rolled his eyes back again, resumed his pose and searched his memory.

"There are strange things done in the midnight sun
By the men who moil for gold..."

"And then I'm gonna need your help," he begged Hester.

She drew up her shoulders, assumed her own pose and continued the poem in a soft singsong, as if back in the Fourth Grade:

"The Arctic trails have their secret tales
That would make your blood run cold;
The Northern Lights have seen queer sights,
But the queerest they ever did see..."

Here Darrow joined in to finish the stanza.

"Was that night on the marge of Lake Lebarge
I cremated Sam McGee."

This time he applauded as Hester curtsied.

When Nate stopped grinning, he assumed a serious countenance. "Only I have to ask, because I've always wondered: How exactly does one 'moil,' and what the heck is the 'marge' of a lake?"

Hester spread her hands apart in an "everyone knows this" expression.

"You know, *moil*. It's like panning for gold. You 'moil' the sand and rocks in your pan. And the marge is the lakeshore, as in 'margin.' It's quite obvious," she sniffed.

"And I'm sure you were a bewitching Fourth Grader," Darrow smiled, taking her hand in his and stretching his other arm comfortably around her shoulders. As his eye wandered across the room it came to a stop at an old clock on Hester's mantel and he came back to earth.

"Oh, criminy, is that the time? I better get on my way, what with your canoe paddling adventure tomorrow," Darrow said, harking back to one of the topics over dinner.

A little sigh escaped Hester's lips.

"So. Detective. I don't know if you've gotten the clue, but you don't really have to make that long trip home," she said, a sapphire sparkle in her eye. "I mean, I have pumped you full of good Oregon wine, and I'd hate for you, as an officer of the law, to get an SUI."

Nate squinted his eyes and cocked his head, struggling to suss it out. "OK, I'll bite. What's an SUI?"

"Stairclimbing Under the Influence," Hester deadpanned.

"Aha," Darrow said, nodding in comprehension, with a small twist of a grin flashing briefly across his face.

He gazed up at Hester's crowded bookcase and momentarily scanned the authors: Jane Austen to Charlotte Brontë to Dorothy L. Sayers to P.G. Wodehouse, their names in gold on wrinkled leather book spines. Puffing out his cheeks, he took a quick sip of the port and turned his eyes to hers in an air of blurting confession.

"Hester, that night we had in February was one of the sweetest I've known, for the spontaneity and the playfulness, and simply the lovely nature of it all – cat vomit aside," he said in a pensive recollection of how Bingle T.'s unfortunately aimed retching had led to his need to get out of his clothes during a previous dinner visit.

"And I can't tell you how much I've thought about it these past few months, and how many times I almost showed up at your door unannounced with a good bottle of bubbly in hopes that you'd say, 'Oh, Nate, how sweet, let's hop in the sack again!' " he said in a rush.

Hester, having just taken a sip of the aromatic ruby liquid, half-choked and almost sprayed her port across the room at this last statement, but Darrow continued before she had a chance to say anything.

"But I also know that there was talk around the department and eyebrows raised about how chummy I'd gotten with a prime witness in a high-profile homicide. And if it had gone up the chain any farther I would so have gotten my butt fired," he said, his eyes riveted now on the cold ashes of the fireplace. "And frankly I'm sorry for being such a coward."

Hester, having regained her composure, took another sip of wine, cleared her throat and mentally chewed on his tone of pragmatic guilt.

"And it's such a cute butt," she said.

Hester was a pragmatist in many ways herself, recognizing that there was no profit in taking insult that Darrow put career over romance.

She silently contemplated his profile and the dark stubble on his sharp jaw line as she poured him another sip of port, nibbled at a crumb of the delightfully spunky cheese, then asked in deliberate provocation, "And speaking of that derrière, you never told me the whole story of how you got the tattoo," she said, humming a quick few bars of "Anchors Aweigh."

It was Darrow's rare turn to lightly blush in Hester's presence.

"Oh. You're talking about my well-anchored personality," he quipped, referring to the anchor tattooed on his right buttock.

Never one to sit still for too long, Darrow sprang from his chair, facing away from Hester, stretching his arms over his head, and then lowering his hands to massage his lower back with an appreciative groan. Slowly his palms wandered lower to cup his own rear end in playful provocation.

Hester didn't pass up the opportunity to give him a swat on the back pocket. "Now stop that!"

He sat back down and hastened to explain.

"I was kind of a basket case the summer after my folks were killed in the car crash. I think I told you about that before." Hester nodded mutely.

"So to get away from the world I'd sailed up the inside of Vancouver Island with my Uncle Babe, from Port Townsend. And one night in Nanaimo I made some friends whose names I will never remember and after a very misguided few hours in a dive bar playing foosball and drinking way too many red beers – the worst thing I can think of now, tomato juice mixed with Pabst Blue Ribbon! – we ended up at a tattoo parlor. I guess I'm just lucky it wasn't somebody's name that I would have to get surgically removed. I can tell you that it was sore as the blazes and Uncle Babe made me sit at the helm for several days in a previously unknown streak of sadism."

Hester bit back a giggle, then leaned over and pecked him on the stubbly cheek. Then it was her turn to turn owlish, peering at the light through her glass of port for a moment before speaking.

"Since it's True Confession night, I will say I had some guilt to work out after our February tryst as well. While I've ridden the Roller Coaster of Love more than once in my day, I am not one to roll in the hay with just any hayseed who comes along, and I admit I hadn't known you for long. So I needed a little time to think about it."

She took another contemplative sip of port and ruefully remembered how alcohol tended to inspire her to mix metaphors.

"And while I did give you some space these past few months, all those times we ran into each other at your favorite pizza joint weren't entirely coincidental. I've eaten more pizza than I've ever had in my *life,* thank you very much. I've had to walk around the Park Blocks twice a day just to keep from becoming a blimp!"

It was Nate's turn to let his eyes wander. The curve of her slim neck, with a few fetching freckles at the base, showed the pizza had done no harm. He leaned over slowly and let his lips nuzzle her left ear.

Hester shrieked in ticklish surprise. "No, not the ear!"

He moved his mouth to her neck and heard an intake of breath. Hester turned her chin and her lips met his. The kiss went on, and on.

Out in the kitchen, Bingle T. was on the windowsill again, his teeth chattering and eyes darting with the movement of a tiny Anna's hummingbird at the feeder a few feet beyond his reach.

This time the cat had nothing to do with the urgent removal of Nate Darrow's clothing.

Chapter Twenty-six

"Why are we having Sunday brunch at a hot-dog restaurant?" Harriet Harrington hissed at her husband.

"It's a little thing I have to do for work, Harriet. You know how you always say you don't want to know the details about my work? Well, let's just say it's one of those times, dear," Harry whispered across the table where they'd just been seated by Gerhard Gerbils, once again clad in his brown jodhpurs. "And they have more than just hot dogs, honeybunch – I hear the sauerbraten and spätzle are good. I have no idea what they are, but I understand they're really quite nice."

When they'd finished their meal and Gerbils brought Harry the check, along with two large plastic bags full of takeout cartons, his wife's eyes opened wide in astonishment.

"Harry, what on earth…?"

"Oh, these are for the *party* tonight, dear. Remember the *party* we're having, with all our friends from my office who love German sausage?" Harry emoted, winking at his wife five times.

"Do you have something in your eye, dear?" she asked, scowling with confusion. Gerbils stared and Harry blushed.

"Just pay the man so we can go," Harriet demanded.

Harry reached for his wallet in the breast pocket of his suit coat but the pocket was empty. He reached for a side pocket with no better luck. Finally after he frantically patted his midsection he found the wallet wedged into the other side pocket.

It was a tight fit in a pocket not usually used for his wallet, and he had to pry it out of the folds. When it finally came, something else popped out, too: a small leather folder containing Harrington's gold-colored detective's shield, with an eagle at the top and "Portland Police" boldly emblazoned on a blue stripe across the bottom.

The folder came to rest atop the restaurant check. The badge stared up at Gerhard Gerbils.

Harry watched Gerbils' eyes flick downward and then back to Harry's face, which flushed crimson.

"Oh, how did that get there, Harriet?" he stammered. "Was – was Junior playing policeman again? You know he really shouldn't, ah, shouldn't leave his toys in Daddy's pockets."

Harriet didn't try to hide her confusion as she picked up her husband's wallet, pulled out a credit card and handed it to Gerbils.

"Would you please just take this so we can be on our way?" she asked, with an air of glacial coolness.

Chapter Twenty-seven

Monday, June 17

"**D**amn and blazes!" Hester exclaimed as her wheeled "trail-along" suitcase tipped over yet again as she tried to drag it over a doorjamb into the bookmobile barn, a garage in a warehouse district near the Lloyd Center mall.

In one hand she gripped a "Gigantor" dark-roast drip from a Jitters Coffee she had passed on Burnside, while she used the other hand to yank the suitcase back upright. Grabbing its leash like a dog walker with a reluctant beagle, she made a beeline for the bookmobile, its shining magenta finish the brightest thing in sight on this gray, overcast morning. On a wall above a stack of oil cans an old clock read "7:20."

"Wouldn't you know our sunny weather would disappear just in time for this ridiculous voyage to the end of the earth?" came Pim's gravelly voice from inside the driver's window, where Hester saw her perched and sipping her own usual morning picker-upper, a mug of hot Postum.

"Oh, Pim, there you are. I'm sorry I'm running a little late," Hester called. "It was just one of those mornings."

"Not a problem, we're still waiting for a couple others. Haven't set eyes yet on Madge O'Hara from Arts and Music. And Sage, the page, had to run back home because he forgot his lucky paddling beret."

Pim paused to take in the full view of her bookmobile colleague, clad this morning in a spotless new pair of ripstop nylon trekking trousers – the L.L. Bean catalog had called the color "schist" – that would convert to shorts when the legs were undone by zippers. Above, a breathable merino-wool T-shirt in "cinnamon," under a khaki safari vest with multiple cargo pockets.

Hester saw Pim's evaluative glance.

"Do you think the T-shirt is OK? I like the merino because it can keep you both warm and cool, depending on the weather, but they only had this one with the figure of Kokopelli on front, and I'm not sure."

Pim, wearing a shirt of mango orange with an image of the fire goddess Pele looking over a field of erupting volcanoes, shrugged. She peered down at Hester's suitcase, then caught the librarian's eye.

"Uh, Hester, you *do* know this is just a day trip, right?"

"Oh, I know, it's just that I haven't been on a canoe trip before, and the weather forecast kept changing, and I wasn't sure just what kind of gear we might need, so I did a little research and the consensus of several adventure authors was that it's better to be overprepared for changing conditions in the wild."

"Ah," Pim said, trying not to smirk.

"And you can take that smirk off your face right now, Ms. Pimala, because when we're out in a squall in the middle of the Great River of the West, you're going to be glad I packed two emergency ponchos so you have something other than that Aloha shirt to ward off hypothermia."

Hester paused to give Pim a playful look of motherly concern.

"Besides, this isn't just gear for the paddle trip. I brought some special Lewis and Clark history books and pamphlets from Grand Central for the bookmobile. I wanted to do a special display when we're in Astoria."

From a knot of people in shorts, sandals and floppy hats at the other side of the garage Candy Carmichael spotted Hester and skipped over to welcome her.

Candy, the library's human resources director, had come to the library a few years earlier from the same Zeus sport-shoe company that was paying the Rose Medallion award. She had yet to "get" librarians. They sat quietly at their desks, didn't make lots of phone calls, and sometimes they even read books during business hours. "What's up with *that*?" she often moaned to the library director.

This was the first time Hester had seen Candy in anything but high-fashion business togs, usually including spiked heels. Today Candy sported day-glo green running shorts on long legs that displayed a from-a-bottle tan. Her also-from-a-bottle blond curls cascaded down over a Zeus hooded sweatshirt in raspberry and mauve bearing the company's hiply abstruse motto, "BE THERE." Completing the outfit: blindingly white knee-high cotton socks and a pair of Zeus multisport high-tops that could have qualified her for the NBA.

It occurred fleetingly to Hester that this outfit was sure to renew whisperings among the staff about Candy's continuing "friendship" with the Zeus CEO, 20 years her senior.

"Hester! Welcome!" Candy gushed, displaying white teeth like piano keys. "We're so excited! I was just over there teaching everyone the Library Cheer! We're going to use it when we need to recharge during our paddle trip today!"

Three large dugout canoes, each carrying eight library employees, were to make the journey, launching around 10 a.m. from the Washington side of the Columbia at the quaint, forgotten-by-time little burg of Skamokawa, its name meaning "smoke on the water" in the Chinookan language.

They would paddle 20 miles downstream and across the wide river to the Oregon side. They aimed to arrive at the historic fur-trading and fishing town of Astoria in time for a midafternoon picnic in a riverfront park with a delegation from the Oregon Library Association's annual convention, being held in nearby Seaside, an old-time beach town replete with penny arcades and carnival rides. Dora, the library's notoriously tightfisted bookkeeper, had approved the whole junket only because it could be charged to the director's rarely-touched budget for "education and conferences."

To Candy Carmichael, this was a trifecta: a team-building exercise that would double as a public relations coup in the final days of the Lewis and Clark-themed Rose Festival, while also showing off the flashy new bookmobile to colleagues from across the state.

She saw the canoe voyage as demonstrating the library's role not only as a repository of history but as a community of scholars who bring history to life, re-enacting some of the final westward miles of the Corps of Discovery.

"And the library is closed Mondays anyway, thanks to the latest levy failure," Pim sniped to Hester.

Carmichael had alerted all of the local TV news directors. A community-college cable channel out of Clatskanie had promised to send an intern to film the launch.

"OK, everybody, listen up!" Carmichael shouted, as the final stragglers arrived. "We have a big day ahead of us! We'll be going in two vans, one of which is towing a trailer with one of our three artisanal dugout canoes on special loan from the Chinook tribe. Plus, as you can see, the other two canoes are coming atop the new Sara Duffy Memorial Bookmobile, which will give us tremendous visibility, so let's all remember that every one of us is an ambassador for the Portland City Library today! We will have TV coverage, so show what a good time you're having! Remember, a smile is just a frown turned upside down!"

Behind her, Hester choked on a mouthful of her coffee, and from the door of the bookmobile Pim mimed sticking her finger down her throat.

Carmichael paused to scan her to-do list, looking like a perky camp counselor, and then looked up with a grin.

"Remember we asked each of you for your shirt size when you were picked for this trip? Well, first thing I'd like everyone to do is go through one of the totes that Linda is unloading from the van over there – " Linda Dimple waved as she hefted another box to the ground " – and find the T-shirt with your name on it. Because we're all part of a team today, tackling a challenging trip, we're going to dress like a team."

At this, Candy unzipped her hoody and pulled it open to show off the bright red T-shirt she wore, bearing the message "WE'RE BOOKIN'" for the Portland City Library."

A mixture of oohs, aahs and muffled groans came from the onlookers as a line formed by the totes.

"And I've been saving this little surprise," Candy continued. "I told you that you wouldn't need to worry about meals. Well, that's because the entire day will be catered by Portland's beloved Wiener Dog Restaurant!"

Just as she finished speaking, a boop-boop-a-doop honk drew everyone's attention and heads turned to the driveway just outside the barn's open bay doors.

Hester gasped as a vehicle shaped like a giant hot dog rolled to a stop. "Oh my gosh, isn't that – the thing that's in TV commercials? Do we get whistles?"

Pim howled with delight.

"No! It *used to be*. The Wiener Dog family bought it surplus a couple years ago, painted the wiener to look more like a bratwurst and added that dachshund hood ornament. Now it's the Portland Wiener Wagen! I saw it last fall at the Clackamas County Fair!"

As she spoke, Gerhard Gerbils, in his lederhosen today, hopped from the driver seat and waved to the assemblage, raising from his bald head a little blue alpine cap with a pink feather on one side.

From the other door came Tony Pucci, the Wiener Dog's lucky, medallion-finding chef, in his kitchen whites and tall toque hat.

"My goodness, I can't believe Mr. Gerbils himself is in on this!" Hester marveled privately to Pim. "I would have thought he'd be in his law office on a Monday."

"Oh, I'm not surprised, Hester. He loves that restaurant, and he knows this is good exposure!"

A half-hour later, the library vans, followed by the magenta bookmobile topped by two dugout canoes, and the garish Wiener Wagen, with puffs of smoke trailing from a little chimney, made a conspicuous caravan as they headed northwest on Highway 30 out of the city.

Nate Darrow and Harry Harrington waved at the entourage as they passed in the fast lane. Darrow craned his neck and a curious look crossed his face as he observed the Wiener Wagen and spied Gerbils and the now-famous cook through its front windows.

A half-mile further on, Harry turned the blue Caprice to take the bridge to Sauvie Island, with a KSNZ news van in hot pursuit.

Chapter Twenty-eight

"This is Misty Day with another KSNZ exclusive, reporting live from the Rajneeshees' Downward Dog Farm on Sauvie Island, where we've followed Portland detectives ready to finally make a bust in the long, drawn-out investigation of the Pieter van Dyke murder," the reporter intoned quietly into her microphone as a live camera followed her to the door of a barn painted with colorful daisies and smiley faces.

Just then the door swung wide and Nate Darrow and Harry Harrington stepped briskly out. Surprised by the TV camera with its red light shining, a murderous look flashed across Darrow's face, quickly replaced by a sinister smile.

"Detective, is it true you've come to arrest Ma Anand Carla, the mastermind behind the Dalles salad-bar poisonings? Is she Pieter van Dyke's killer?" the reporter blurted before Darrow could speak.

The off-kilter smile stayed pasted on the detective's face.

"Misty, why don't you come inside and question Carla yourself?" he asked, taking her by the elbow and forcefully ushering her into the barn before she could respond.

The camera feed continued on screens of KSNZ viewers all over Portland, with the electric banner "Live police bust on Sauvie Island," as the image jogged and bumped into a hay-filled stable.

At the edge of a stall, a man with mutton-chop sideburns and a wary-eyed, dark-haired woman with a ferret-like face and denim coveralls looked up curiously from where they sat on bales of hay next to a little horse and two tiny colts that bore a striking resemblance to Jack Russell terriers.

"Detective, what on earth?" asked Dr. Nigel Hartley, the veterinarian Nate and Harry had met on their last visit to the island.

"Sorry for this intrusion again, Doctor Hartley, but after the little demonstration you and Carla just gave, I happened to run into my reporter friend and I thought she'd want to show her viewers how you folks are teaching these clever little horses to be service animals."

"Oh, yes, it's really quite amazing what smart creatures these are," the vet said. "Carla, why don't you continue the exercise?"

Ma Anand Carla knelt in the hay, gazed into the little mare's big brown eyes and asked, "Rainbow, can you count to three? THREE, Rainbow?"

Carla knocked her knuckles on the wooden floor of the barn three times, knock-knock-knock. As if in reply, the little chestnut horse raised her own hoof and repeated the rapping, KNOCK-KNOCK-KNOCK.

"Good girl, Rainbow!" cried Carla, offering a handful of alfalfa to the horse, whose tiny colts now cavorted at her heels.

Darrow spoke up, turning his head to be sure the camera would catch his words.

"So, Doctor, I understand that Carla suggested this training the night she spent with you and her fellow farmhands when these colts were born – the same unfortunate night that Pieter van Dyke died?"

"Yes, Detective, Carla said she could sense Rainbow's natural intelligence and urged that we consider enrolling the horse in the service-animal field for which she developed a passion during her unfortunate incarceration."

"And these little horses even get outfitted with special little tennis shoes and wear harnesses just like a seeing-eye dog!" piped up Harry Harrington, who had thought the whole idea ludicrous at first but was newly won over.

Misty Day, ever the stage-wise professional, now elbowed her way back in front of the live camera.

"And there you have it, Thad and Marilu," she purred to the News Break anchors watching from the downtown studio. "A tale of misguided suspicion on the part of the police turned to a heartwarming conclusion – a story of rehabilitation and hope. Live from Sauvie Island, this is Misty Day."

In the background, car doors slammed. Nate Darrow and Harry Harrington were already back in the Caprice, headed for the city.

Chapter Twenty-nine

After crossing the Lewis and Clark Bridge to Longview, Washington, the library caravan followed Highway 4 downriver, through the little burg of Skamokawa to the launch site at Vista Park, where Steamboat Slough and Skamokawa Creek branched off from the Columbia River.

The community's main buildings were a riverfront inn, the last remaining authentic steamboat landing on the Columbia, now on the national historic register, and Redmen Hall, an old fraternal lodge with a politically incorrect name that was now a museum.

For breakfast, Gerhard Gerbils distributed a Kielbasa-on-a-Stick to each of the crew, and while sitting on a gray drift log next to the launching ramp Pim managed to spray her red T-shirt with yellow mustard.

All was proceeding normally.

"This isn't quite what the real Corps of Discovery had to eat," announced Sage, the page, in his high, nasal voice, as he sat in the lotus position atop a riverbank stump surrounded by weedy willow trees. Sage, a painfully thin, goateed Reed College dropout of about 19 with jet-black hair to his waist and a single emerald stud piercing his nose, fancied himself a critic, be it of food, theater, literature or life. For this trip, his hair was in two long braids, which he thought suggestive of a Chinook brave. Others saw him differently.

"It's like he's a tall, dark Pippi Longstocking," Pim whispered to Hester.

While Sage's comment was nothing more than a bored dig at the world, it was taken as a challenge by three Reference Line workers perched together on a nearby boulder who had been answering Lewis and Clark trivia questions ever since Rose Festival opened.

"Actually, a sausage encased in buffalo intestine was a favorite preparation of their guide, Toussaint Charbonneau, who called it boudin blanc," said Jeannette Nelson, a tall and lean woman with salt-and-pepper shoulder-length hair and a perennial scowl.

"But on this stretch of the river they'd have almost certainly have been eating wapato, a starchy potato-like root that was a staple of the Chinook tribe," chirped Debbie Wilkes, whose mousy-brown pixie haircut framed a cherry-cheeked face.

"That is, of course, if they hadn't traded for a fresh dog from one of the tribal villages," added Eva Temple, a Hillary Clinton look-alike, giving a smug, self-satisfied look over the top of her tiger-striped reading glasses as she paused from reading a slim volume of Baudelaire. "In fact, dog was a coveted staple for the Corps of Discovery by this late juncture in their hardscrabble voyage across an unforgiving wilderness."

At this pronouncement, several of the group paused to look skeptically at their half-eaten kielbasas.

"Well, they do often call this sort of thing a hot dog," Linda Dimple said with a gulp.

"Oh, don't worry, they only make the best German sausage at the Wiener Dog!" Pim reassured her.

"Sorry, did you not want a historical précis on the Corps of Discovery diet?" Jeannette asked, pointing her thin nose at Sage, who was yawning widely. "Maybe you were just making idle conversation."

Sage gave a nervous chuckle and pointed his forefinger at his nose to affirm the latter.

At this juncture, Candy Carmichael strode over from where she had completed supervising the unloading of the canoes with the help of Bob Newall, the maintenance man, who had ridden along and would drive the bookmobile down Highway 4 and across the four-mile-long Astoria-Megler Bridge to meet them in Astoria.

"OK, listen up everyone!" Candy shouted, straining to be heard over a breeze that had come up out of the west. "We'll need to average about 5 miles per hour in order to get to our destination in time for the picnic the Wiener Dog will provide for us and other library guests in Astoria. And that will be a special treat! Thanks to some strings pulled by our own Ethel Pimala, we've obtained an old family recipe from a gentleman who is a direct descendant of Toussaint Charbonneau, an actual member of the Corps of Discovery. So our picnic dinner will be…" Here she stopped to study a clipboard " – a special sausage called boudin blanc, with a side dish of wapato, which I'm told is like a Native American potato!"

All around, the group shared stunned looks.

Linda Dimple finally broke the silence in a small voice. "Do you think they'll use real buffalo intestine?"

"I thought it was a salmon barbecue!" whined Jeannette Nelson.

"At least it's not roast rack of spaniel," Sage wisecracked.

Hester, taking comfort in knowing of a few good restaurants in Astoria, quietly sang,

"You say to-MAY-to, I say to-MAH-to,
You say po-TAY-to, I say wa-PAH-to…"

She stopped when Pim gave her the stink eye.

Candy, oblivious of the rumblings in the ranks, continued down her list of announcements.

"And as you might know, we have the benefit of some leadership today by Vance Boylston, from the accounting office, who grew up on Lake Oswego and has paddled a canoe there since he was in diapers, to hear Vance tell it. Please give him your full attention as he tells a little about our route today and goes over some safety tips."

Boylston, a fair-skinned, carrot-topped lump of a man who wore his official Assistant Scoutmaster shirt from Troop 72, demonstrated how to put on life vests and spoke for five minutes about paddling technique, how to balance the canoe and strategies for a man-overboard rescue.

"And I think our best route today will be to cross the river immediately, over to some of the protected sloughs on the far side, out of this weather that seems to be blowing up. The main thing is to get well out of the ship channel!" he bellowed, trying to be heard over the rush of wind that continued to build.

"What did he say?" Hester asked Pim, who was preoccupied with cinching a drawstring to keep her woven pandanus hat from blowing away.

"Something about how we should get well out in the ship channel!" Pim said distractedly.

Hester mulled this advice. "Oh, I guess that's how we catch the best current. That makes sense."

Boylston concluded by passing out a folded paper to the designated lead paddlers for each canoe. For Hester and Pim's canoe, this was Sage, the page, who had won the honor because of his long arms. Pim had already privately nicknamed him Wilt the Stilt.

"I'm proud of saving the library some money on this endeavor," Boylston explained smugly. "I was in Astoria for a conference last week and my favorite restaurant, the Pig 'n' Pancake, had this map of the Lower Columbia on their paper place mats. After my group finished breakfast, I collected all the place mats! I know it doesn't have a lot of detail, but it ought to get us there."

Hester looked at him in alarm.

"Well, let's hope no killer reefs or giant whirlpools are covered by a gravy stain or a blot of jelly, Captain Cook!" she said under her breath.

Chapter Thirty

"Pull! Pull! Pull!"

Sage's nasally voice didn't exactly inspire a Gold Medal performance, Hester thought as she dipped her paddle into the cold and murky green water of the Columbia.

She and Pim were in the last boat of the lineup heading out from the entrance of Steamboat Slough into the wide waters of the main river at 10:20 that morning.

Hester felt a sense of foreboding as they rounded a point of mossy rocks and suddenly got a full view of the mighty river. It quickly widened from what reasonably looked like a *river* to a four- or five-mile-wide windswept tideland pocked by sandbars and edged by coastal hills and wild, undeveloped shore. Not far downstream, a thick band of fog split the river midstream. It looked like it was blowing their way.

And while the whole idea of these dugout canoes, each created from a single log of Western red cedar and with a carved wolf head at the prow, was excitingly historical, Hester could already tell the thin neoprene pad they'd each been given to kneel on in the rough-hewed vessels wasn't going to stop her from being bruised like a bad banana tomorrow.

As they left the slough's entrance and headed out into the river, choppy waves acted like a tractor beam, slowing the canoes.

Pim, just in front of Hester in her canoe's lineup, was immediately struggling.

Hester noted that the short and stout bookmobile driver was having trouble holding the paddle as they'd been instructed, with one hand on the top of the shank and the other just above the blade. Her arms just didn't reach. Without proper positioning she wasn't getting leverage on the paddle, which kept glancing off the water's surface instead of digging deep as they'd been instructed. At one point, Pim almost lost her grip on it entirely. Hester could see Pim's frustration quickly mounting.

And an additional problem soon became apparent. Not only were Pim's efforts for naught, but several of the dugout's strongest paddlers were paddling on the opposite side from her. As a result of the imbalance, their canoe had soon veered sharply to starboard, pointing downstream toward a prominent landmark a few miles off called Pillar Rock, which poked up out of the river some 100 feet offshore.

Sage, whose lucky beret had slipped down over his eyes, seemed oblivious. Hester saw it was time to take charge.

"Does anybody see where we're going?"

"Pull! Pull!" Sage's coaching was sounding more and more like some sort of mewling waterfowl.

"I think we might need to balance out our paddlers," Hester called, craning her neck to try to catch Sage's attention.

Her word of caution was drowned out by an ongoing travelogue by the three women from Reference Line, who sat between Sage and Pim.

"Did everybody know that Pillar Rock was originally some 75 feet higher before it was altered and flattened to position a navigational marker at its top?" Jeannette Nelson announced as if emceeing a pageant.

"And that Lewis and Clark camped onshore within sight of the rock twice on their journey?" Debbie Wilkes added.

"In fact, that it was from that campsite that Clark penned the giddy and famously wrong pronouncement, 'Ocian in View!' because the river became so wide and wild, even though they were still some 20 miles from the sea?" Eva Temple concluded in authoritative triumph.

"OK, thank you, Noble Oracles! Now STOP PADDLING!" Hester shrilled.

Suddenly it was quiet and still. Necks craning, all eyes turned her way.

"It's just that – look, the others are going that way, and we're veering back toward shore," she explained, nodding toward the other canoes, already some distance off and making quick progress toward the middle of the river.

There was some debate over simply reassigning paddling sides, but Jeannette Nelson complained that she couldn't switch because she was very strongly left-handed and that she had faced discrimination and bullying over it all her life.

Candy Carmichael, sitting in the rear, agreed to trade sides with Linda Dimple, but while Eva Temple insisted she was ambidextrous and would swap sides whenever needed, she reserved the right to take frequent breaks because her bursitis was flaring up again.

To be sure the balance was right, Sage decided, he would stand in the bow and look back to observe as they all took their best strong paddle stroke.

And, of course, when the canoe suddenly thrust forward, he fell overboard.

It was to their credit that the ladies figured out how to counterbalance the narrow canoe while Jeannette and Debbie, who regularly spent their lunch hours power lifting at the downtown Y, hauled him back aboard.

He was quickly shivering in the cool breeze, and low scudding clouds gave no promise of a warming day. Hester handed Sage a Haystack Rock souvenir beach towel she'd stashed in a dry bag, and he wrapped himself up in it, looking surprisingly like Sacajawea with his braids protruding as he settled back in his paddling position at the bow and looked out to find the other canoes.

Where the other canoes had last been seen a half-mile off, a giant ship, riding low in the water from the weight of thousands of raw logs stacked high on its deck, plowed a four-foot bow wave as it headed downstream en route to Japan.

Once the ship passed, that snaking band of fog – the "smoke on the water" for which Skamokawa was named – now obliterated their view of anything beyond.

They were as alone as Lewis and Clark felt 200 years earlier.

Chapter Thirty-one

"**S**o, Nate, can you picture some blind guy in line at Safeway with My Little Pony clomping its hoof on the linoleum 46 times to tell him how many cents he should be getting from the change machine?" Harry Harrington asked with a howl as they sipped cappuccinos during a break at Jitters Coffee Co.'s Northwest Portland café.

Darrow was shaking his head with a wry smile when a buzzing like an angry hive of bees sounded from the pocket of his houndstooth-checked jacket.

"Yikes, I keep experimenting with different rings on this phone but I'm not sure that's the one yet," Darrow exclaimed as he dug for the gadget.

Fiddling to raise the antenna and peering to punch the right button, he finally yelped into the mouthpiece: "Nate Darrow!"

Leaning close to the earpiece, Harry could hear the caller identify himself as Ranger John Vouri from Fort Vancouver National Historic Site. Then came a few exchanges of more muffled conversation that included several comments from Darrow such as "Really?" and "You're sure?"

When Darrow signed off, he picked up his coffee and sipped at it with a distant look in his eyes while Harry stared at him like a cat waiting for a canary to fly his way.

"So?!" Harry finally cajoled.

Darrow responded by looking vacantly Harrington's way, then picking up a little wooden stirring stick that sat in a small pool of brown liquid next to his cup and rapidly stirring his drink until all the foam dissolved into the coffee.

"Earth to Nate! Earth to Nate!" Harrington heckled.

"Oh. Harry." Finally his eyes focused on his partner. "That was the ranger from Fort Vancouver, the one who had been to his father's funeral."

Harrington nodded expectantly.

"Um, well, it seems he's back now."

Harrington threw himself back against his chair and groaned. "Yes, I got that much, Nate. So what did he say?"

"Hmm, I'm trying to figure out what it means."

"Nate! Give!" Harrington spoke in clipped syllables, like a trainer instructing a show dog.

Darrow looked at him from heavy-lidded eyes. "Well, it seems the old French pistol *was* returned to the library on time, according to arrangements this Vouri fellow made by phone from Ohio with one of his assistants."

Harry jutted his chin out while he thought about this for a moment.

"So that confirms that van Dyke, not Charbonneau, had easier access to the weapon!"

Darrow nodded.

"But there's something else. Vouri also says that because of the potential for accidents, he's absolutely meticulous in tracking which of the re-enactment replicas is loaded with blanks for use in skirmishes and which is loaded with live ammunition to be used in target shooting."

Harrington was turning red now. "Yeah? And?"

"Well, apparently this pistol was loaded for target practice but wasn't fired before Vouri got the emergency call about his father. In fact, he's quite worried now that in all the confusion the pistol was returned to the library without proper 'decommissioning,' as he describes it." Darrow pinched the bridge of his nose and shook his head as he concluded.

Harry looked like a gasping salmon that had just been pulled off the gaff hook. Then the significance of what Darrow said dawned in his eyes.

"Nate, you don't mean…"

Darrow still pinching between his eyes, nodded now.

"Whether Pieter van Dyke knew it or not, that antique pistol he took to the park was likely loaded and ready to fire."

Chapter Thirty-two

"So Charbonneau may be telling the truth and the pistol could have been fired without any help from him," Harry Harrington speculated as he and Nate Darrow walked down 23rd Avenue past the late breakfast crowd gobbling Eggs Benedict in the window at Papa Haydn's Cafe.

"It sounds that way, though my buddy Pomp is far from guilt-free in all this."

Hunched against the morning's unexpectedly cool wind, Darrow jangled change in his trouser pocket as they waited for a light to change, then spoke again as he and Harry crossed Kearney Street toward the parked Caprice.

"But if Pomp is to be believed, someone else happened upon van Dyke after Charbonneau had left him, removed the Rose Medallion that Pomp had left on a ribbon around his neck, then fired the pistol into van Dyke's heart. Then whoever the killer was apparently threw the pistol into the creek – to be found by a fisherman – and the medallion into the bushes, to be found by a sausage-loving dachshund."

"A sausage-loving dachshund owned by the victim's law partner and escorted by his soon-to-be son-in-law," Harry pointed out as he unlocked the driver's door of the car, parked in a "police only" slot by the red-brick façade of Good Samaritan Hospital, at 23rd and Lovejoy.

"Yeah, that's a coincidence I don't like at all," Darrow sighed, folding himself into the passenger seat of the car just as a horde of angry bees drowned out his words.

"Darrow!" he shouted, after a few moments of scrambling to pull out his phone.

This time he didn't keep Harry guessing at the end of the phone call.

"That was the lab. We might have hit pay-dirt on my wild hunch about the sausage grease on the Rose Medallion. It will take a few days for DNA testing to be positive, but Don Finkle says he can state with 75 percent certainty that the grease found on the medallion came from the kitchen of the Wiener Dog!"

Harrington gave a long, low whistle.

"Way to go with the hunches, Nate, even though I thought Harriet was going to have my cojones with brown mustard on a kaiser roll yesterday!"

Darrow was back in remote mode, staring vacantly at the front veranda of a new-age bookstore across the street in front of which two of the youngest Rajneeshees from Sauvie Island were passing out carnations to passers-by.

When Nate spoke again it was as if snapping out of a trance.

"So, Harry, that day when the Rajneeshees were in the park feeding squirrels and Schnitzel the wonder dog supposedly chased a squirrel into the bushes and came back with the medallion, maybe it wasn't such a surprise to Tony the cook."

Harrington was struggling to keep up with the thought process.

"You mean because…"

"Exactly. Because Tony the cook had smeared sausage grease on the medallion before hiding it in those bushes so everyone would watch Schnitzel find it, steering suspicion away from him by making an adorable animal story out of what had been a grim murder investigation!"

Behind his glasses, Harry's eyes opened wide.

"And thanks to the reward money Tony is now partners in his restaurant, not just the flunky boiling bratwurst! Nate, we gotta talk to this guy!"

Harry turned the ignition and wheeled the Caprice into traffic as he reached for the mike on his police radio and started to report their destination as the restaurant at Jantzen Beach.

"Hold on, Harry, hold on. He's not there today."

"Not there? How do you…"

"No, apparently he's down on the Lower Columbia somewhere – feeding hot dogs to Hester and her library friends, if I'm not mistaken," said Darrow, recalling that morning's colorful caravan on Highway 30.

Darrow pulled out his phone.

"Let me find out just where they went, and while I do that, you get us headed toward Astoria!"

Chapter Thirty-three

"**W**here did they g-g-go?" asked Sage, the page, his teeth chattering from the cold wind on his dripping braids as he scanned the wide and misty river for the other canoes.

"Oh, goodness, they were just there! Just before that ship passed," Candy Carmichael spoke up from the rear of the dugout. "But hold on, that's why we brought the walkie-talkies! In case we got separated!"

In the interest of cultural authenticity and self-reliance, Carmichael had forbidden the paddlers from bringing cellular phones on the trip. But some type of communication was needed in case of trouble. She pulled a palm-sized radio from a jacket pocket, peered at it and twisted a knob to turn it on. It gave a beep. Poking at a button, she spoke.

"Canoe Three to Canoe One, Canoe Three to Canoe One, come in Canoe One!"

All they heard was static.

"This is some new gadget Vance picked up at Radio Shack. Does anybody know anything about these things?" Candy asked in disgust.

The Three Oracles, as Hester had come to think of them, tended to take such questions too literally.

"The Federal Communications Commission authorized the new Family Radio Service as an improved walkie-talkie radio system using channelized frequencies around 462 and 467 megahertz in the ultra high frequency band," responded Jeanette Nelson.

"It does not suffer the interference found on citizen's band radio at 27 megahertz, or on the 49 megahertz band also used by cordless phones, toys and baby monitors," added Debbie Wilkes.

"FRS radios function on 14 channels, and individual handsets must be tuned to the same channel in order to communicate," Eva Temple chimed in, turning to give Candy a skeptical glance over the top rim of her glasses. "I don't suppose you and the other geniuses agreed on a channel before leaving the shore?"

Candy gave her a dirty look, frowned and punched some more buttons. The radio beeped and squawked.

Pim, never one to suffer fools gladly, groaned. "Why don't we just paddle the goldurn boat? That Vince guy said we should stay in the shipping channel – to catch the current or something."

"Yes," Hester piped up. "I vote we follow that ship! We're bound to see the others when the fog lifts!"

So they paddled. To the good, the exercise helped warm them up. Pim soon grew more accustomed to the regular strokes. Eva's bursitis seemed to ease. Sage's teeth stopped chattering.

So when they finally passed Pillar Rock, he showed his good spirits by bolting to a crouch in the bow of the dugout, emoting with a hand shading his brow, gazing into the distance and shouting, "Ocian in view!"

And then he fell overboard again.

The spirit of re-enactment paled quickly after the second man-overboard drill, just about the same time the sky grew darker and whitecaps started roiling the water. The paddlers labored on silently, still looking for the other canoes ahead, while taking turns digging out jackets and sweatshirts in an effort to stave off goosepimples caused by the rapidly dropping temperature. Hester finally spoke up again.

"Does anybody know what it means when the waves start breaking on top like that? And is it just me or does it seem like we're not moving ahead anymore?"

"On the Beaufort scale, whitecaps generally begin when the wind reaches a velocity of 10 to 12 knots," Jeanette answered.

"And small-craft navigation on the Lower Columbia is often complicated by tidal action during a flood tide that actually reverses the river's flow as far as 25 miles inland from the mouth," Debbie declared.

"OK, STOP!" Hester commanded. "I mean…" She took a deep breath. "Thank you, ladies."

She rested her paddle and watched the droplets of water stream off its end into the river, an inky green now that the sky had become gloomier overhead. Then Hester raised her head, turned back to the organizer of the day's voyage and spoke in a calm voice that belied her thoughts.

"And Candy, might I ask how carefully we consulted the tide tables before setting out today?"

Candy Carmichael's face twitched three times before she answered.

"I…I went up to Science and Business and asked about currents and they came up with some equation and said something like the currents 'would *really* be in our favor when they were in our favor,' which I took to just be some kind of librarian doublespeak. I mean, of course, the current would be in our favor. We're going downstream! It's a river!"

The seven other paddlers returned dark stares in her direction.

At the same time, the wind began to gust, sending salty spray in their faces and rendering further conversation pointless. Without prompting, everyone in the canoe started paddling, just to help steady out their craft in the bouncing water.

It soon became evident they weren't going to make it to Astoria. With the rolling fog and wind-whipped water, it was hard to see *where* they were going. But the winds and currents were obviously deciding their course for them. Paddling toward the river's center, toward Oregon, their progress quickly stalled and their paddles thrashed the water with little result. Paddling for the Washington shore, they drew steadily closer to a high banked beach.

Onshore, trees were beginning to sway. It occurred to Hester, and the realization seemed reflected on the grim faces of her weary crewmates: With the weather deteriorating, they could be battling for their lives if they didn't soon reach the beach.

Time condensed. Muscles ached and hands grew numb, but finally their bow crunched against the pebbly shore. They dragged themselves out of the dugout, now filled with puddles of water, and staggered to safety. Hester and Pim gave a hand to Sage, who was shivering and pale, and they all plopped down on a bleached gray drift log against a high bank covered with amber-colored sea grass.

Eva Temple, who'd replaced her Baudelaire with a small digest of William Clark's journals before leaving shore, pulled the volume from a fanny pack and studied it wordlessly while the others looked on in exhausted silence, their arms clasped around themselves against the cold. She unfolded a map and wrestled with it as it flapped in the wind. She peered downriver, toward a mist-shrouded bridge about a mile away, and then spoke with conviction to her seven companions.

"When Lewis and Clark hit this stretch of river the Corps of Discovery ran into weather much like this. And much like we just experienced, their canoes were driven ashore. They were trapped for six miserable days by winds and waves at a spot that Clark in his journal called a 'dismal little nitch.' "

She paused, as if for dramatic effect, once again gazing around her with weary eyes.

"Well, ladies – and gentleman – we're having one hell of a re-enactment. From what I read and what I see on this map, I'm pretty certain this is the place. Welcome to Dismal Nitch!"

Chapter Thirty-four

In November 1805, Clark in his journal described Dismal Nitch as little more than jagged rocks and a steep hillside that prevented the Corps' escape from a narrow strip of beach. Wind-driven waves pummeled the beached canoes and endless rain punished the explorers, whose leather clothing by this time in their journey was rotting on their backs.

The good news for the band of weary librarians: Two centuries had transformed the landscape, pretty much leveling the high bluff and turning Dismal Nitch into a minor historical site, complete with a highway rest area and a fishermen-tramped path that led down to the beach.

"Oh saints be praised, look up there, do I see restrooms?" Hester called, rallying the morale of the windblown crew just as big raindrops started to splatter on their foreheads.

"I got first dibs on the electric hand dryer," Linda Dimple shouted, showing a burst of speed up the path that Hester wouldn't have thought possible in a children's librarian little taller than the average attendee of her Saturday morning story hour.

Pim, always practical, recruited the Three Oracles to help her pull the canoe up the beach and tie its bow line to a log. Seeing the walkie-talkie Candy Carmichael had left on her seat, she popped it into a pocket for safekeeping. Then they all trooped up the path and took shelter in the public restrooms, gathering curious looks from a carload of tourists from Boise.

Candy Carmichael, reasserting her authority, spied a pay phone next to an information kiosk, collected spare dimes from her cohorts and was soon on the line with Bob Newall, one of the few library employees who had been issued a cellular phone.

Bob had taken the bookmobile to the waterfront park in Astoria where the Wiener Wagen was setting up for the afternoon picnic. The other two canoes had arrived safely a short time earlier, he said.

"They caught the counter-current through the sloughs on the Oregon side and made fantastic progress – they hardly had to paddle at all!" Newall said. "In fact, I heard one of them say it was like having a little outboard motor on their transom!"

Carmichael, deciding not to pass this latter news on to her paddling colleagues, soon convinced Newall that the Canoe No. 3 crew needed rescuing.

"I can get someone to bring one of the vans for the crew, but that darn Lars Simpson was driving the van with the trailer and he took a load of library folk out to Seaside to ride the bumper cars," Newall said. "I think there was some kinda challenge between the Periodicals Department and Government Documents."

"Bob, I don't care if the whole bleeding staff has gone off to Cannon Beach for pony rides, we just need some help over here!"

"But I'll have to bring your canoe back, too, don't you see?" Newall spluttered. "Those are valuable artifacts and my friend Lester Fishhawk from the Chinook tribe will skin me if anything happens to that canoe! I guess I'll have to bring the bookmobile over and we can hoist it on top."

"OK, whatever, but please get over here as soon as you can. One of our crew fell overboard twice and I think he's in a bad way. And Bob? Get the Wiener Dog people to send over some food and hot coffee when you come!"

Chapter Thirty-five

By the time the lead canoes arrived at Astoria, Gerhard Gerbils and Tony Pucci had erected a red-and-white striped dining tent over a row of picnic tables in a waterfront park next to the maritime museum.

In a tarped shelter, Pucci had two cooking fires going with black iron tripods for hanging pots. Part of what won the Wiener Dog the catering contract for the outing was the promise of this effort at historical authenticity.

The windblown alder smoke mixed with the smell of beach kelp from the brackish waters of the river estuary to give the whole park a sort of wilderness perfume that riffed off the character of Astoria's old gray fishing piers and cheap motels.

When Bob Newall sounded the alarm about the crew stranded at Dismal Nitch, Gerbils volunteered to make the 15-minute drive across the bridge in the Wiener Wagen.

"That's the easiest way to get some food and hot drinks over to them, and Tony can't leave the wapato now that he's got it in the Dutch ovens," Gerbils explained.

Besides which, he told Newall, he'd taken some first-responder medical training in his younger days when he'd climbed Mount Hood, and that might come in handy.

Newall waved Gerbils on his way across the river, along with Ralph O'Sullivan, one of the library drivers, at the wheel of the second van.

The Astoria-Megler Bridge, carrying two lanes of U.S. 101 across four miles of water between Washington and Oregon, is one of the man-made wonders of the Lower Columbia. With a cantilever-truss design in a 200-foot high section allowing oceangoing freighters to pass beneath it near the Astoria shore, it appears to soar right out of a hillside of Victorian homes in the town that was founded just a few years after Lewis and Clark paddled these shores. The roadway actually reaches the high arch via a corkscrewing ramp branching off the town's main drag.

The Wiener Wagen could be seen winding its way up the approach ramp as Nate Darrow and Harry Harrington pulled to a stop in the park next to the bookmobile. Their Caprice was tilting like a drunken sailor, riding on what Harry scornfully called a "pony tire," the undersized spare with which most modern automobiles now come equipped.

Running over a four-inch nail on Highway 30 near the river town of St. Helens had necessitated a tire change, slowing their arrival and putting Harry in a grumpy mood.

"Why anybody thought this kind of piss-ant equipment was an acceptable idea for a law-enforcement vehicle is beyond me, and besides it's just plain embarrassing," he was grumbling to Darrow in a broken-record rant that had given Nate a headache for the last 30 miles. "I'm just glad the local tire shop said they could fix us up with a replacement while we're here. I mean, what if we had to do a high-speed pursuit after some hopped up Mustang on the way back to Portland? It says right on the side of that little pony tire, 'Do not exceed 45 miles per hour'!"

Darrow nodded for the umpteenth time, but his attention had shifted to Bob Newall, who perched atop the magenta bookmobile. On its side, the airbrushed face of the old librarian seemed to smile with an unnerving smarminess. Darrow noticed that her eyes seemed to follow him as he got out of the Caprice and approached the big bus.

Newall was working with some ropes to lash one of the dugout canoes to a rack atop the bookmobile. Darrow called a greeting and flashed his badge, and Newall scampered down a stepladder.

"What can I do for you, officers?" said Newall, wiping his wind-burned hands on the tails of his plaid flannel shirt and introducing himself with a friendly handshake.

"We're detectives, actually, down from Portland." Darrow craned his neck and caught sight of the chef working over the fires by the wind-ruffled dining tent. "We're making some inquiries and need to talk to some people who came along on your trip today. I just saw the Wiener

Wagen heading across the bridge, but I see the cook is still here. What's going on?"

Newall explained the emergency on the other side of the river.

"And I need to head over there in a minute, too, with old Bessie here, to retrieve their canoe, though how I'm going to hoist it up on the roof I'm not sure. I got that one up there with the help of some big burly pages who are used to ferrying boxes full of books, but those guys took off on a toot to Seaside, and the folks stuck at Dismal Nitch are mostly the delicately nurtured sex – not that I'm one of them anti-feminine pig types, but you get my drift."

Darrow listened to this monologue in silence. After looking around quickly to get a look at the few remaining library staff who sat at the picnic tables under the tent, he asked, "What about Hester McGarrigle and Ethel Pimala? Have you seen them?"

"Oh, they're part of the Dismal Nitch crew! But I don't think either of them really has the muscle to hoist one of these dugouts. Pim is quite the little fireplug, I grant you, but the woman isn't any taller than a Smurf! And Ms. McGarrigle has the height, but with due respect I think there's more brains than brawn there!"

Darrow shot Newall a sideways look, then chewed his thumbnail for a moment as he looked out at the stormy river and made a snap decision. He stepped aside for a moment for a word in his partner's ear.

"Harry, I'm going with Bob here. Maybe I can help with the canoe, and perhaps get a word with Mr. Gerbils and see what he knows. I know you want to stick around for the guy from the garage to come with that new tire, so why don't you keep our friend, the cook, company."

At this, Harry brightened.

"Nate, you know I'm the barbecue king! I bet they're doing salmon!"

Chapter Thirty-six

Hester never thought she'd be so glad to see a motorized vehicle shaped like a 27-foot bratwurst.

But as she munched a footlong hot dog with sauerkraut and sipped a scalding coffee under the eaves of the Dismal Nitch Rest Area restroom, she felt her energy seeping back.

Meanwhile, Gerhard Gerbils was in the library van taking Sage's pulse, while Ralph O'Sullivan wrapped the wet paddler in an old blanket found under a seat in the back of the van.

"You say he fell in *twice*?" Gerbils asked Candy Carmichael.

"Yes, he seemed to have a special talent for it," the H.R. director said drily. "He was shivering earlier, but that stopped so we thought he was OK."

"I recall them saying shivering sometimes stops as hypothermia progresses. His pulse seems weak and I don't like how blue his lips look. Sage, do you recall what date this is?"

The young man slowly opened his eyes and thought for a moment. Looking across the parking lot, he saw a small Ford stop in front of the restroom building. Two old-fashioned Dominican nuns, in full black and white habits, got out and headed inside.

"Is it, like, Halloween?" he asked groggily.

Gerbils exchanged an alarmed glance with Carmichael. "You need to get this young man to the Emergency Room in Astoria."

Candy Carmichael, for all her failings in preparedness, snapped into action now.

"OK, everybody into the van!" she hollered, adding a shrill tweet on the emergency whistle attached to her life vest.

Hester, dreading the thought of spending time in close quarters with the bearer of that whistle, stepped up. "Candy – Pim and I are OK, why don't we wait for the bookmobile and we'll be sure the canoe is secure?"

"OK, good idea, Hester! Ralph has a cellphone, so we'll call Bob and tell him you're waiting," Carmichael called back, shepherding the Three Oracles and Linda Dimple into seats and pulling the door closed behind her just as the van took off with a spray of gravel. Knowing Ralph O'Sullivan, who occasionally subbed for Pim as the bookmobile driver, Hester sensed that his only disappointment with the situation was that the van had no siren.

When the van disappeared down the road, Hester turned back to see the two nuns quizzing Gerbils about the Wiener Wagen, then posing for photos in front of it. She and Pim took the opportunity to step into the restroom to change into some dry clothes Hester had stashed in her dry bag.

In the echoing tile restroom, as the two colleagues wriggled out of wet socks, Pim confided with Hester about their week.

"I gotta say, this is turning into the crappiest June we've had in years. First the bookmobile overheats in the parade, then we run over the president of the library board, and now your Inspector Clousseau has his suspects all wrong. Hester, I *know* Pomp didn't do it. He had no reason to kill Pieter van Dyke. Maybe he has a quirky sense of humor but this isn't him. I've been watching Perry Mason reruns for 30 years and I know, when there's a murder, you follow the money. And nine times out of 10 it leads you to a spouse or partner! That's where I'll tell your Inspector to look – the spouse or partner!"

Hester mulled this over.

"Well, Pim, I can't get past the idea that something about the Rose Medallion might still give some useful clue. I'm going to urge Nate Darrow to look more closely at the medallion," she said as they exited the restroom and almost ran into Gerhard Gerbils, drinking from a water fountain just outside the door.

"Oh, excuse me, Mr. Gerbils! I didn't see you there!" Hester exclaimed.

She caught an odd look in his eye as Gerbils stepped quickly out of the way, then stood staring at them, as if about to speak, but unable to find words.

"Gosh, I never thought I'd be rescued by the Wiener Wagen!" Pim finally said to break the awkward silence. "I just love it! Oh, Mr. Gerbils, would you take a picture of me and Hester in front of it?" She pulled an old Instamatic camera from a pocket.

Gerbils smiled and came out of his trance as he took the camera from her.

"OK, say 'bratwurst,' " Gerbils clowned as he snapped their photo.

"Well, there's no reason we have to stand outside in the cold," he said as he handed the camera back to Pim. "Would you like to see the inside?"

Pim's beaming smile served as her answer.

Gerbils used his keys to open the cockpit door and held it open, waving an arm for Hester and Pim to climb aboard.

❖

As Bob Newall steered the lumbering bookmobile into the truck parking for the Dismal Nitch Rest Area, Nate Darrow was curious to see the Wiener Wagen careen out of the parking lot and on to the highway, passing them in the direction of Astoria. The ungainly vehicle swerved so violently to avoid the bookmobile that the giant fiberglass wiener was wagging a bit.

"Jeez, what's his hurry?" Darrow wondered aloud.

It took only a few moments of looking around the restrooms and a glance down at the lone canoe on the beach to realize that Hester and Pim were gone.

Newall looked confused.

"I don't understand – That call from Ms. Carmichael said they'd wait here. And I can't believe they left that canoe unattended. It's a valuable artifact!"

Just then a crackling of static and a series of beeps came from Newall's shirt pocket. He reached down and pulled out a twin of the walkie-talkie Candy Carmichael had carried. As he turned up the volume now, a voice issued loudly from the speaker.

"Help, we're hostages in the Wiener – "

Then the radio went silent. Newall's jaw dropped as his eyes met Darrow's.

"That was Ethel! That was Ethel Pimala, I'd know her voice anywhere!" Newall croaked.

"Let's go!" Darrow cried, turning back toward the bookmobile. But Newall froze.

"I can't leave that canoe there, the waves will carry it off! It's a museum piece – "

Darrow didn't hesitate. He stepped back and grabbed the walkie-talkie and Newall's keys from his hand.

"OK, you stay with the canoe. If I can drive Orvald's old Volvos, I can drive anything!"

Bob Newall stood and stared as rain started to pelt harder and the Miss Sara Duffy Memorial Bookmobile lurched out of the parking lot, stalled once, then careened toward the Astoria bridge.

The late librarian's eyes seemed to look back accusingly as the big bus disappeared in a cloud of purple exhaust.

Chapter Thirty-seven

Gerhard Gerbils wasn't going to chance another stunt from the bookmobile ladies after the short, husky one had tried calling for help. So he finished taping their wrists behind their backs using a roll of book tape he had spied in one of their purses.

"I'll never again call that 'the librarian's friend,' " he heard the tall librarian whisper bitterly to the other.

What to do next?

Gerbils had never been a star at strategy. It was why he'd never shined as a courtroom lawyer. Behind-the-scenes procedures and strongly worded letters were more his forté.

He trusted nobody had heard the few words broadcast before he'd snatched the radio away. When the tall, younger woman wouldn't stop protesting, he'd stuffed kitchen rags in each of their mouths. Unfortunately he couldn't find clean ones so both of the women were gagging slightly from the sauerkraut juice the rags had mopped up after an earlier spill.

Nothing for it, Gerbils thought as he climbed back in the driver's seat. If they'd just behaved and kept quiet, they wouldn't have a problem.

He'd stopped the Wiener Wagen on the narrow shoulder of the bridge about a mile from the Washington shore. This section of the bridge roadway was low, only 6 feet above the water. The bridge wasn't much wider than the two lanes of traffic it carried, one in each direction, so cars zooming past had to veer out into the oncoming lane. But one advantage to driving the Wiener Wagen: It caught the attention of other drivers. There was no need to put out flares. Most passing motorists honked and waved at what Gerbils had once seen ignominiously referred to – in its previous corporate life as a symbol of one of America's biggest hot dog makers – as "a rolling tribute to pig lips and chicken necks."

As he put the ungainly vehicle back into gear and got it moving again, he pocketed the vintage Luger he always kept in the glove box as a deterrent to what he mirthfully called "wienerjacking."

"In all seriousness, this is a valuable classic vehicle, you never know what crazy carjackers might try," he'd told Tony Pucci only that morning.

In any case, the old German pistol that once belonged to his grandfather had helped him keep the librarians from escaping.

Now, the same can't-miss-it factor that made the Wiener Wagen such a public-relations wonder was perhaps his biggest problem. What kind of getaway car was this? Not only was it less anonymous than driving a nuclear missile-launcher through town, it was built on an old motorhome frame, so it wallowed around corners.

Again with the not thinking ahead, he grumbled, mentally kicking himself.

And what was he going to do with the librarians? He had no idea.

But after overhearing their conversation at the restroom he couldn't let them go their merry way. How could he make anybody understand what had happened between him and his law partner that night in the park?

If he could just get back to town before the alert went out, maybe he could ditch the Wiener Wagen, rent a car – steal a car? – and head for Mexico. Or at least some little rental cottage on the coast where nobody would find him until he worked out a better plan. Until he figured out how to prove his innocence?

"What am I doing? What am I doing? Ach du lieber, what am I doing?" Gerbils moaned aloud. On the wide bench seat next to him the two women's eyes showed as white as shucked oyster shells.

Just then the walkie-talkie Gerbils had stuffed in a cup holder crackled to life.

"Pim! Hester! It's Nate Darrow. I'm right behind you! Mr. Gerbils, please pull over and I'm sure we can talk this out! The state police are on their way. There's no place to go!"

Panic flashed across Gerbils' face. He grabbed the Luger from his pocket and punched the accelerator to the floor, sending the Wiener Wagen rocking wildly in the wind.

Chapter Thirty-eight

The brightly colored bookmobile was a quarter-mile behind the garish Wiener Wagen with its bulbous, red-flecked bratwurst riding high atop a golden bun.

All Darrow could do was hold his foot to the floor and hope the roaring diesel engine had guts. Slowly, he was gaining on them. Behind him, books flew to the floor each time the big bus tipped in the wind. Several times, river water flew up on the roadway and splashed across the bookmobile's windshield as if tossed from a bucket, sending Darrow frantically searching for the wiper switch.

His mind was strangely detached as he willed the bookmobile forward. Looking out at the broad vista of gale-thrashed water and misty hills, he could make out the river bars called Desdemona Sands. A buddy who had taught Nate celestial navigation had run aground there when heading out to sea in his home-built sailboat. Adept at reading the stars but not so good at the world in front of his nose, he thought with a thin smile. He felt that way himself sometimes.

Forcing his mind back to the road, he saw the Wiener Wagen start uphill as the bridge gradually rose toward its high arch. Stuck momentarily behind a slow and laboring old Volkswagen microbus, the hot dog on wheels finally pulled out to pass. The pause was what Darrow needed to close the gap.

"I can ketchup, I know it!" he said aloud. It was hard to avoid hot-dog humor.

As the bookmobile rocked into the oncoming lane and barreled past the old VW, Darrow flashed the headlights and blew the air horn in hopes of getting Gerbils' attention.

"Meep, meep," answered the VW.

Finally the bookmobile pulled within feet of the wind-wagging wiener, which showed no signs of pulling over. The speedometer read 65. Darrow worried that the corkscrew turn at the end of the bridge might be too great a test for Gerbils' driving skills.

"That could be a turn for the wurst!" he blurted out loud, quickly chagrined that too little sleep and too much coffee had brought out his inner 12-year-old.

Reminding himself that Hester and Pim were in danger, Darrow punched the accelerator to the floor again and pulled the magenta bus up next to the speeding Wiener Wagen just as the two ungainly vehicles crested the bridge's 20-story-high arch.

Looking over, Darrow waved his arm to signal Gerbils to pull over.

Darrow could see the wild-eyed sausage king look sideways, like a glance from a nervous racehorse. A glimpse of red hair beyond the bald head told him Hester was there.

Whether from a pummeling wind gust or an intentional swerve, suddenly the Wiener Wagen locked mirrors with the bookmobile and bits of brightly colored fiberglass went flying. Screeching like 500 fingernails on 500 chalkboards filled Darrow's ears as the sides of the two speeding vehicles ground together.

Heart pounding, Nate hit the brakes and swerved the bookmobile back into the right lane as the Wiener Wagen bolted ahead.

"You're not going to do anybody any favors if we all end up going off the bridge," Darrow chided himself, with a frightening flashback to how his parents died – when their car flew off this same Highway 101 into Washington's Hood Canal some 18 years earlier.

"Just give him room," Darrow whispered, lifting his foot from the accelerator.

Darrow watched the bookmobile's speedometer sink to 40 as the Wiener Wagen disappeared into the now-driving rain.

❖

As he rounded the first curve of the corkscrew ramp, Gerhard Gerbils gripped the wheel like Captain Ahab battling the white whale.

The Wiener Wagen lifted its wheels on one side but stayed upright. Behind the cockpit, condiments flew across the galley Gerbils had added to the exotic vehicle.

Far below, in the distance, a flotilla of speeding cars with flashing blue lights was splitting traffic through downtown Astoria. They were coming his way.

Hester and Pim, helpless to hold on, slid back and forth across the bench seat. Gerbils fought to push them away as he struggled for control.

As the Wiener Wagen rounded the final downward curve to intersect with the highway through town, Hester watched with alarm as the traffic signal turned to red in front of them.

Gerbils wasn't stopping.

Like a bobsled out of control at the bottom of its course, the giant hot dog shot into the intersection. From the corner of her eye Hester saw a speeding log truck. She yelled through the folds of moist towel. An air horn blasted without end.

Then everything was spinning.

Chapter Thirty-nine

Where they lay a foot from each other on the wet asphalt, under the glare of headlights from cars stopped at every which angle in the roadway, Pim and Hester opened their eyes almost simultaneously. As they'd tumbled like wet laundry in the crash, the tape had slipped off their wrists.

They each reached slowly up and pulled the kitchen rags from their mouths.

The first sense Hester perceived was a terrible headache. Dizziness. Then, surprisingly, a sweet, spicy smell.

She watched as Pim's eyes came slowly into focus. Then shock and alarm played across her old friend's face.

"My God, Hester, you're hurt! Your chin!" came Pim's raspy words as she struggled to sit up, wincing with the effort.

Hester put her hand to her jaw and with a sense of unreality felt a sticky wetness. Seeing a red smear on her fingers, her heart pounded with the realization that she was injured and bleeding.

But wait. She touched her fingers to her tongue.

"Ketchup!" she cried.

A stocky policeman was suddenly hovering over her, telling her not to move. Another cop, skinny and with a crew cut, was tending to Pim.

Looking at her bruised colleague, who would clearly have two black eyes, Hester strained to understand what she was seeing. What terrible internal injury caused yellow oozing? The Aloha shirt Pim had changed back into at Dismal Nitch was now covered in –

"Mustard!" Hester realized with a relieved sigh.

❖

Two hours later, an Oregon State Police cruiser dropped Nate Darrow off at the park next to the maritime museum, where a luscious, meaty aroma carried on the smoky breeze.

The afternoon sky was now a mix of puffy white cumulus and occasional patches of blue, what Darrow's mother used to call "Dutchman's pants." Summer weather seemed to be on the way back.

As Nate strode toward the dining tent where a few straggling library staff still visited at picnic tables littered with crumpled napkins and soiled paper plates, he saw Harry Harrington wearing a white apron and the chef's toque earlier sported by Tony Pucci. Harry was poised with a large meat fork over a smoking campfire.

Pucci sat at a picnic table nearby, handcuffed to the table frame.

"Hey, Nate, you're just in time for the last serving of Toussaint Charbonneau's boudin blanc!" Harrington called out to him. "But I'm afraid the wapato was toast an hour ago. Those Dutch ovens get hot sitting right in the embers."

Darrow mutely held out a plate while Harrington speared two large sausage links from a huge cast-iron skillet.

"How are they?" Harrington asked.

Darrow, ravenous after the long day, swallowed a bite before speaking. He knew Harry wasn't asking about the sausage.

"Pim broke her collar bone – a hairline thing – and Hester has a severe concussion, and they both have lots of nasty scrapes. But they were all pretty lucky, considering. Gerbils broke a leg. They're all staying the night at Columbia Memorial."

"How about the truck driver?"

"A bump on the head. Even his Kenworth came through with only a few scrapes. But the Wiener Wagen will roll no more. It was a clean slice. One end of the dog was on the south side of the road, the other on the north. The vehicle frame was intact, but the fiberglass body just broke into pieces. And there were condiments everywhere!"

As if in proof, Darrow pulled a slightly squashed squirt-bottle of mustard from his coat pocket. He untwisted the pointy cap and drew two precise lines of yellow down the length of his sausage and then took another bite.

While chewing, he tilted his head toward Pucci with a questioning look at Harry.

"Oh, our friend there?" Harrington responded. "Well, we started chatting over the campfire after you left and it wasn't long until I asked him about how the sausage grease got on the Rose Medallion, at which time he decided to audition for the 100-yard dash. Luckily I'm no slouch with a Frisbee, or in this case a Dutch oven lid. Caught him right in the back of the knee and it was quite the merry mix-up of limbs as he went down. You can see how he got an unfortunate grass stain on this nice white apron – "

Harry held out a corner of the apron he wore.

"But I figured it was less messy than shooting him, and saved me a whole lot of lousy paperwork. Kinda burned my fingers, though," he said, shaking his hand in the air.

Darrow listened with bemusement. Once again, he saw new depths in Harry Harrington.

Peering at Harry's fingers, Nate instructed, "Here, hold your hand out. This is a Darrow family secret cure. Where does it hurt?"

Harry held out three fingers and Nate squirted yellow mustard on the burned fingertips.

"REALLY? Nate, don't mess around."

"I'm not kidding. Just leave it there for five minutes and then tell me if it still hurts."

"This sounds like some kind of New England witchcraft thing with your family."

"Hey, Mom came from old Salem. We never used the 'W' word in our home. She was an herbalist, that's all."

"Well, my family came from Salem, *Oregon,* where chamomile is a weed and wheat grass is stuff you feed pigs." Harry kept a skeptical cast to his eye. Darrow chewed.

"Well, we got the new tire on the car," Harry finally added. "Again, we can drive with dignity."

Darrow nodded and gave a small grin as he finished the last bite of his second sausage, then gazed for a moment at Tony Pucci, who sat just out of earshot with his head cradled on one elbow, looking miserable.

"So did the Galloping Gourmet over there give any hints about who did what and why?"

Harrington reached over and used a long stick to poke at the remains of one of the bonfires until he brought a log back aflame, then raised a foot on the picnic bench next to Darrow and shook his head.

"After I Mirandized him, he clammed up at first. I think he was hoping his future father-in-law would come back and give him some legal advice. But he heard about the accident at the same time the Astoria cop came by to tell me, and he got a little chatty after that. Insisted he knew nothing about van Dyke's murder, but that Gerbils had been searching for the medallion all week and found it 'under a bush in the park,' so he said. But, the cook says, Gerbils realized that whoever turned in the medallion would become a murder suspect. So he came up with the idea of smearing it with sausage grease and having the dog find it, with a little help from the cook. And the cook's reward for keeping quiet and handing over the $50,000 reward would be a partnership in the restaurant, along with marrying into the family."

Darrow rolled his eyes. Then, spotting an insulated picnic jug at the end of the table, he grabbed a paper cup from a stack and worked the jug's tap to get some lemonade, which he drank in one gulp.

"Well, part of that sounds plausible, but it doesn't explain why Gerhard Gerbils kidnapped two library workers and drove his Wiener Wagen into a load of old-growth Doug fir."

He threw the paper cup on to the fire and watched it flame.

"In any case, we have Mr. Pucci on obstruction of justice, unlawful flight and possibly animal cruelty."

At Harrington's look of confusion, Nate elaborated.

"Feeding a dachshund a steady diet of sausage grease can't be good for it."

As Harry untied the apron and pulled off the chef's hat, Darrow asked, "How are the fingers?"

Harry held up his hand, fingers splayed wide, and stared. Most of the yellow mustard had soaked into his skin.

"You know, I'd forgotten all about the burns," he said in wonder. "I guess – I guess your mother *mustard* known something about first aid!"

Darrow winced.

Harrington looked thoughtful for a moment, then added, "Come on, let's hit the road. I don't *relish* being late for dinner."

"OK, OK, I realize this case is going to be haunted by hot dog jokes, so just get them out of your system now!" Darrow protested.

Harrington gave an innocent look.

"*Frankly*, Nate, I don't usually indulge in that kind of low humor. But if you really want a joke contest, I say let the *wiener* take all."

Darrow, walking away toward the Caprice, waggled his fingers back at Harry in a 'bring it on' gesture.

"I have to say I never *sausage* a miracle cure for burns!" Harrington hollered after him, pausing just a moment before adding, "My fingers don't hurt a *teeny wienie* bit!"

Nate Darrow opened the passenger door of the car and climbed in with his index fingers plugging both ears.

Chapter Forty

Friday, June 28
Twelve days later
Portland

Nate, Hester and Pim gave a welcoming smile as their waitress deposited two galvanized buckets of steaming butter clams and a pitcher of Henry Weinhard's on their table at Pal's Shanty, a Sandy Boulevard institution famed for its hot bivalves and cold beer.

"Do you need any help getting the clams out of the shells?" Hester asked Pim, who still had some bandages under her Aloha shirt to immobilize her healing clavicle. Today's shirt was fuchsia with images of the Pan Am Clipper flying over Mauna Loa.

"No, I think I can just about manage this, but this achy old shoulder is probably going to help me forecast the weather any time it gets damp," she grumbled. "Maybe it will give me an excuse to move back home to a warmer climate – someplace with law and order, where library folks aren't getting themselves killed all the time, and the wrong people don't keep getting arrested for it!"

Darrow's eyes met her glare for a moment. He let her approbation wash away with a long swallow of cold beer.

"And how's your head, Hester?" Darrow inquired as he used a fork to pluck a clam out of its shell and dunk it in a bowl of drawn butter that the server had set down next to a jar of Dijon mustard, Darrow's other favorite clam dip.

"Well, Dr. Patel in Astoria told me in no uncertain terms that I should never play football again," she replied with a note of irony, popping a clam in her mouth and chewing for a moment. "He informed me, in the most precise medical terms, that I had 'rung my gong good.' But the headaches have eased and I'm sleeping better, thanks."

Pim drained her glass and held it out to Darrow for a refill. "And how's Mr. Gerbils? Have they moved him from the hospital to the jail yet?"

Darrow refilled glasses all around as he answered. "He's going to be under guard in a rehab unit at Providence for a while yet. He broke his left tibia in two places, but he's on the mend."

Hester scooped a portion of Caesar salad onto a plate and popped a deliciously soggy crouton into her mouth before squaring eyes with Nate in a no-nonsense look.

"So, how much can you tell us? What was this all about? Once again, I think we've earned an explanation."

Darrow, remembering Hester's brave leap from the careening bookmobile and Pim's mistaken incarceration during his last investigation of a library murder, gave a small nod and an ironic grin. "Yeah, you two need to pursue quieter lives. This bookmobile business is dangerous."

Pim flattened her mouth and peered over the top of her cateyes at him. Darrow shifted his eyes between the two determined women and waved a hand in surrender.

"OK, I'll tell you on a confidential basis, but this is under a total Cone of Silence."

"You can always trust Agent 99," Hester replied, raising her right hand with her fingers splayed apart in a Vulcan "Live Long and Prosper" salute. Hester, who spent much more time as a child reading books than watching what her father called "the boob tube," tended to mix up pop-culture TV references.

"OK, Inspector," Pim reluctantly responded, crossing herself as if about to say confession.

As a delaying tactic, Darrow quickly speared clams from three shells, collecting them on his fork like a shish kebab, swabbed them in Dijon and hungrily wolfed them down. He took another swallow of the beer and then sat back and crossed his arms and legs.

"Mr. Gerbils is working a deal with the prosecutor, so he's told all. He admits he shot Pieter van Dyke but he claims it was an accident."

"Oh, my!" Hester exclaimed, letting her fork drop on the table. Pim took off her glasses and stared open-mouthed.

Darrow nodded.

"His story is that he was legitimately searching for the Rose Medallion. His restaurant is in financial trouble and the prize money was enough to cover a loan that was due. Without help, he stood to lose his business."

"And he loves that restaurant, it's his family heritage, it would be like – like the Partridge Family losing their bus!" Pim contributed. At this, Hester looked mildly confused.

Darrow slurped some beer and forged on.

"He had overextended himself with debt. He had sunk more than $100,000 into the Wiener Wagen alone. Anyway, he says he had made a special arrangement with a former client, a guy who drives an Oregonian delivery truck, to read him the medallion clue around 4 o'clock every morning, at the start of his run. Well, that morning, only a few dozen papers had come off the press before it broke down, but Gerbils' guy still came through, so Gerbils was definitely the only person in Portland with the clue before 10 o'clock. So he was the first person in the park and found van Dyke staked out in the horseshoe pit the way Charbonneau said he left him – cold and shivering but alive."

Pim gave a self-righteous snort. "I told you Pomp wasn't a killer!"

Darrow poured her some more beer.

"So there was van Dyke, in just his underpants, with his hands and legs duct-taped to horseshoe stakes and his mouth duct-taped, with the Rose Medallion on a ribbon around his neck and the old French pistol sitting on his belly where Charbonneau had left it."

Darrow took a sip of beer to moisten his tongue. Hester took a nibble of salad, scooping up Parmesan on top of a romaine leaf.

"But when Gerbils pulled the tape off van Dyke's mouth, apparently van Dyke assumed Gerbils was in on the whole thing and began shouting all sorts of nasty things about Gerbils' heritage, calling him a Nazi torturer and that sort of thing."

Pim looked affronted. "But the Gerbils family fled Germany to get away from the goose-stepping morons!"

"And few things more infuriate a righteous man than being called a traitor to his cause – a mutineer!" Hester interjected. "It's – it's like 'Billy Budd.' Melville!"

Pim and Darrow exchanged shrugs, and then nodded as if they knew what she meant. It was their best defense when Hester got literary.

Darrow, flinging empty shells into a discard bowl in search of more clams, continued.

"So Gerbils says he reacted badly and without realizing he'd picked up the pistol he was waving it at van Dyke and telling him to shut up, that his father resisted Hitler's goons and was a hero in his day. And he says the pistol went off by accident."

Hester and Pim, until then sitting on the edges of their chairs with palms covering their mouths, simultaneously drained their glasses. Darrow waved to the passing waitress and pointed to the empty pitcher with a beguiling smile. She scooped it up to get a refill.

"And could we get a basket of that Parmesan garlic cheese bread?" he added.

Hester squinted her eyes in thought.

"OK, the obvious question: Why didn't Gerbils just call for help? Maybe some paramedics could have saved Pieter! And Gerbils is a lawyer, he should have known that turning himself in would be for the best if it really was an accident."

Darrow rolled up a lettuce leaf and ate it like celery between sentences.

"Well, I think you know about the mountain-rescue training he'd had. In fact, the doctor in Astoria said Gerbils deserved credit for sending your hypothermic page to the E.R. He said that kid could have died without the right care. And old Gerhard claims he tried to give van Dyke CPR but that he pegged out almost immediately, and Gerbils said he knows how to read a pulse. He says he just plain panicked – that there were headlights coming toward the park and he was sure other medallion hunters would be there soon because the clue was so easy. So he grabbed the medallion, chucked the pistol in the creek and ran."

Pim gave a low whistle, using her good arm to pour beer for everyone from the newly arrived pitcher. "Anybody for shuffleboard?" she asked, eyeing the indoor court next to the pool tables at the far side of the tavern.

Hester and Nate acted as if they hadn't heard.

"So what about the cook?" Hester wondered.

"He got lured into it by the promise of a partnership with his future father-in-law, and it seems he really didn't know how Gerbils had come by the medallion. He's agreed to plead guilty to a minor fraud charge and he'll probably get off with a suspended sentence and some kind of probation."

"But so much for his bright future with the restaurant," Hester observed. "I hear Zeus Shoes stopped payment on the $50,000 medallion reward, and I doubt anyone blames them."

Darrow, dipping a hunk of cheesy garlic bread in the remaining clam nectar, gave a sardonic smile.

"Well, it has come to light that Gerbils, the efficient German lawyer, had already filed the partnership papers. And Wiener Dog Inc. had an $85,000 insurance policy on the Wiener Wagen, because it really was a valuable collector's vehicle, and Gerbils had inserted all sorts of obscure legal language to the effect that, although the premium was helping to bankrupt him, the policy would pay off in just about any circumstance, no matter who was to blame."

Pim was scowling. "What's that all mean, in English, Inspector?"

"It means that the insurance money should give Tony Pucci enough to pay off the creditors and keep the restaurant afloat after all, even if his father-in-law is locked up. Which might not even happen, if the German lawyer's lawyers are good."

Hester's mouth suddenly formed an "O" as an alarming thought occurred to her.

"You don't think he meant to total the Wiener Wagen, kill himself – and *us*, I might add – and give his daughter and her future hubby a happily-ever-after in the process?"

Darrow's eyes smoldered, staring across the room at a trio of laughing pool players as he considered Hester's theory.

"Suicide by motorized hot dog? I think I'm going to ask him exactly that, and maybe spread the idea around the prosecutor's office before they settle on any plea bargain."

Pim, arguing that her aching shoulder required "a good liquid painkiller," had poured herself another schooner of beer.

"One thing I'm still wondering about, Inspector," she said, stifling a small burp and sounding slightly tipsy now, "is the Rajneeshees. They kept popping up like whack-a-moles in this whole doggone business. What the hey-nonny-nonny was up with that?"

Hester chimed in. "Yes! There was even one of them on the Macarena cruise! And what about the coincidence of Ma Anand Carla being released just in time for Pieter van Dyke's death? Mr. Gerbils even warned us about her!"

"Gerbils admits that was just to send us off on a wild-goose chase. And ladies, I know this goes against everything you learned from every murder mystery you ever read," Darrow explained in syrupy tones, giving them his best basset-hound eyes. "And I doubt I'll ever convince our esteemed police chief. But," he concluded, now feigning a Hercule Poirot French accent, "Sometimes a coinci-*dence* is just a coinci-*dence*."

With a self-satisfied air of having wrapped up the case, Darrow dipped another piece of cheese bread in clam nectar. But Pim wasn't about to let Darrow off too easily.

"OK, Inspector, but what about another life you've ruint? I swear, you're like that Mr. Toad. We used to read about him in the kids' story circles, how he sped recklessly across the countryside without giving two hoo-ha's about the destruction in his wake."

Nate looked at her like she had toads crawling out of her ears.

"I'm talking about Pomp Charbonneau! What happens to my friend Pomp?"

"Ah. The wild offspring of Sacajawea."

Darrow finished chewing and swallowed before continuing.

"Well, Ethel, Mr. Charbonneau isn't exactly guilt-free in all this. There's the question of counterfeiting a U.S. postage stamp, though he'll probably skate on that. It's a little too esoteric for the prosecutors. But he is plainly guilty of some sort of assault charge for leaving Pieter van Dyke trussed up like a Thanksgiving turkey in his skivvies, not to mention the damage to his poor old landlord's tractor out in Washington County."

Pim nibbled on a piece of cheesy bread, took a swig of beer and belched unabashedly in Darrow's direction.

"Pim! What would your mother say!" Hester scolded.

"Barge coming through?" Pim responded, drawing back her cheeks, crossing her eyes and sticking her tongue out the side of her mouth in a Harpo Marx imitation. Hester slid the beer pitcher away from Pim's end of the table.

Darrow chuckled and continued.

"But because Pomp came clean and helped with our investigation in the end, I don't think a judge will go too hard on him and his oddball practical jokes. Last I heard, he was going up before old Judge Augustus McGillicuddy, who has something of a screwball sense of humor himself. Remember that UFO nut who was arrested for faking crop circles with his old dump truck in a strawberry patch out near Amity? The guy was a few sheets to the wind and never thought about how the tire tracks were a bit of a giveaway. Judge McGillicuddy, who is a bit of a strawberry shortcake fan, wasn't about to let the poor fool off with just a fine, though. So he sentenced him to four years on litter patrol. Behind his back, the prosecutors call him 'Garbage Gus.' I suspect Mr. Charbonneau could be looking at a lifetime of picking up candy wrappers along the Sunset Highway, but he'll probably be back for your re-enactments at the fort."

Darrow paused to drain his glass, then continued as another thought struck him.

"He may have to look for a new job, though, after messing around with the Rose Medallion clue. *The Oregonian* takes the medallion pretty seriously."

Hester rolled that over in her mind, then remembered a bit of news she had to share with Nate and Pim.

"Oh! I forgot to tell you both – and to thank you, Nate! You have saved Portland from the gimlet eye of Miss Sara Duffy!"

Darrow's eyebrows knit as Hester laughed.

"Do tell?"

"Yes! When you were riding to our rescue and you sideswiped the Wiener Wagen on the Astoria bridge, the impact scraped Miss Duffy's face off one side of the bookmobile. And Dora, the library's delightfully cheapskate bookkeeper, has found that it's thousands of dollars cheaper to have the whole bookmobile repainted than to have any of the fancy supergraphics restored. So we're getting our plain old magenta bookmobile back!"

"Hallelujah!" responded a broadly smiling Pim, who was never a fan of the late head librarian and had made it no secret that she thought the new bookmobile's outer decor was "as cheesy as Tillamook." She happily pounded on the table with her good hand.

On the table, Pim's fist caught the handle of a butter knife. Its blade rested under the edge of one of the clam buckets. The bucket flipped up, crashed on its side, knocked over the mustard jar, which caught an edge of the butter bowl. A torrent of Dijon, clam nectar, half-coagulated butter and empty shells cascaded into Nate Darrow's lap.

Darrow leapt to his feet, sending clamshells flying, and looked down in shock at the brownish yellow starburst across the front of his khaki trousers.

For a moment Pim looked like a deer in headlights, frightened at what she'd done.

Then, gradually, an impish look crept across her face.

"Well, Inspector," she quipped, looking down proudly at her for-once spotless Aloha shirt. "Looks like lunch is on you."

Appendix

Candy Carmichael's Library Cheer

Where do you get
great books to read?

Portland City Library!

Need answers to questions
in the nick of time?

Portland City Reference Line!

Can't come to us? We'll
come on wheels.

Portland City Bookmobile!*

*Hester always hated the last line
because it didn't rhyme properly.

Hester's favorite dessert recipe

Nana's Cream Puffs

Preheat oven to 400 degrees F.

Heat to a rolling boil in a saucepan:
1 cup water
½ cup butter

Stir in all at once:
1 cup sifted flour

Stir vigorously over low heat until mixture leaves the side of the pan and forms into a ball – approximately 1 minute. Remove from heat and beat in thoroughly, one at a time:
4 eggs

Beat the mixture until smooth and velvety. Drop by rounded tablespoonful onto a baking-paper-lined baking sheet. Bake until dry, approximately 45-55 minutes.

Custard filling

Mix in saucepan:
1 cup sugar
1 teaspoon salt
2/3 cup flour

Stir in:
4 cups milk

Cook over medium heat, stirring until it boils. Boil one minute. Remove from heat. Stir a little over half of this mixture into:
8 egg yolks (or 4 whole eggs), lightly beaten

Blend the mixture back into the saucepan. Bring just to the boiling point
(Continued on next page)

and then cool. Blend in:
4 teaspoons vanilla

Thin chocolate icing

Melt together over hot water:
1 square unsweetened Baker's chocolate
1 teaspoon butter

Remove from hot water and blend in:
1 cup sifted confectioners'sugar
2 Tablespoons boiling water

Beat until smooth.

To assemble the cream puffs:

Slice the top off a cooled cream puff. Gently pull out any soft strands from the interior. Fill with custard. Replace top and spoon thin chocolate icing over the top. If icing gets too thick, add a few drops of boiling water to it. Refrigerate cream puffs. Enjoy.